KU-225-975

Contents

A Note About The Author

Ian Lancaster Fleming was born on 28th May 1908 in London. A newspaper journalist and a writer, Fleming created one of the most famous characters in twentieth-century fiction – James Bond.

Ian Fleming came from a wealthy family and was educated at Eton – a famous private school for boys. While at Eton he met another boy called George Scaramanga. Fleming named the main villain[1] of *The Man with the Golden Gun*, Francisco Scaramanga, after this boy, with whom he is said to have fought. After he left Eton, he trained to be a soldier at Sandhurst Military Academy. However, after less than a year there he left and went to Europe, where he studied languages at Munich and Geneva universities.

Fleming's first job was as a journalist in the Soviet Union. From 1929 to 1933, he worked in Moscow for a news agency called Reuters. While he was employed by this organization, he learnt about Soviet spies who were involved in selling intelligence – government secrets – to other countries. Fleming sent reports about these spies and the related court trials to Reuters in London. When he returned to London in 1933, he worked first as a banker and then as a broker – an agent who buys and sells goods for other people.

During the Second World War (1939–1945), Ian Fleming became an officer in the Department of Naval Intelligence, at the headquarters of the British Navy. He was the assistant to the Director of Naval Intelligence, who was responsible for employing spies and gathering intelligence for Britain. As part of this work, Fleming travelled to many countries and organized secret operations against Britain's enemies. It was his experience in this job that would later provide inspiration for many of the characters and incidents that he wrote about in his Bond books. Once the war had ended, Fleming then worked for *The Sunday Times* newspaper.

At the age of nearly 44, while staying in Jamaica, he began to write about spies and dangerous criminals. In 1952 he completed his first novel, *Casino Royale*. In the same year, he married Anne Charteris, and his only son, Caspar, was born.

Casino Royale was the first in a long line of adventure stories about a handsome British secret agent called James Bond. Bond was a spy who had a taste for danger, women, fast cars, gambling[2] and good food and drink. Each of the Bond books Fleming wrote detailed a different mission that the secret agent had been given to complete. James Bond had a 'licence to kill', which meant that sometimes he was told to kill his enemies.

Casino Royale was very successful and the adventures of James Bond, agent number 007, became very popular. By the time Fleming died on 12th August 1964, more than forty million copies of the James Bond books had already been sold. The books are: *Casino Royale* (1953), *Live and Let Die* (1954), *Moonraker* (1955), *Diamonds Are Forever* (1956), *From Russia with Love* (1957), *Dr No* (1958), *Goldfinger* (1959), *For Your Eyes Only* (1960), *Thunderball* (1961), *The Spy Who Loved Me* (1962), *On Her Majesty's Secret Service* (1963), *You Only Live Twice* (1964), *The Man with the Golden Gun* (1965) and *Octopussy and The Living Daylights* (1966).

The first Ian Fleming book to be made into a film was *Dr No*. The film was first shown in 1962 with Sean Connery starring as James Bond. The film *The Man with the Golden Gun* was released in 1974. It was only loosely based on the original plot and starred the actor Roger Moore. By 2012, seven different actors had played the part of Secret Agent 007. The Bond films continue to be huge international successes. Millions of people all over the world have seen and loved the films of Fleming's books.

A Note About The Story

The story of *The Man with the Golden Gun* takes place in the early 1960s. Since Fleming wrote the story, the names of some of the countries and their kinds of government have changed.

In October 1917 there was a revolution in Russia and a communist government came into power. These communists believed that everyone in their country had to share everything – money, power and land. Russia joined with the other countries it now controlled to form the Union of Soviet Socialist Republics (the Soviet Union).

During the Second World War, France, Britain, the United States and the Soviet Union fought together – they were allies. But soon after the Second World War, nations around the world who believed in democracy[3] became allies with the United States and Western Europe. Meanwhile nations who believed in communism became allied to the Soviet Union. The United States and the Soviet Union both began to build huge numbers of powerful weapons, including atomic bombs[4]. The Soviet Union had a special secret police force called the KGB. It was the role of KGB officers to protect the interests of the Soviet Union and collect intelligence about its enemies.

For forty years each group of countries watched the other. They did not fight each other, but each side looked for ways to make life difficult for their enemies. This period – 1945 to 1989 – was called the Cold War.

Ian Fleming's stories are set during the Cold War. It was a dangerous time and many people were frightened that the next war would involve atomic bombs. As a result they loved to read Ian Fleming's exciting adventures about secret missions, some of which involved spies trying to kill each other.

Most of the story's action takes place on the Caribbean island of Jamaica. During the last year of the Second World War, Ian

MACMILLAN READERS

UPPER LEVEL

IAN FLEMING

The Man with
the Golden Gun

Retold by Helen Holwill

UPPER LEVEL

Founding Editor: John Milne

The Macmillan Readers provide a choice of enjoyable reading materials for learners of English. The series is published at six levels – Starter, Beginner, Elementary, Pre-intermediate, Intermediate and Upper.

Level Control

Information, structure and vocabulary are controlled to suit the students' ability at each level.

The number of words at each level:

Starter	about 300 basic words
Beginner	about 600 basic words
Elementary	about 1100 basic words
Pre-intermediate	about 1400 basic words
Intermediate	about 1600 basic words
Upper	about 2200 basic words

Vocabulary

Some difficult words and phrases in this book are important for understanding the story. Some of these words are explained in the story, some are shown in the pictures and others are marked with a number like this: ...³. Phrases are marked with ᴾ. Words with a number are explained in the *Glossary* at the end of the book and phrases are explained on the *Useful Phrases* pages.

Answer Keys

Answer Keys for the *Points For Understanding* and *Exercises* sections can be found at www.macmillanenglish.com/readers.

1

'Can I Help You?'

Everyone thought that Commander James Bond, one of the best agents in the British Secret Intelligence Service, was dead. A year ago the Head of the Secret Service, who was a man known only by the initial 'M', had chosen Bond to go to Japan on a highly important mission. His task had been to gather secret information from the Japanese about the Soviet Union. But the job had gone badly wrong and Bond had become involved in a dangerous battle with a known criminal called Blofeld. It was thought that Bond had killed Blofeld, but no one knew what had happened to Bond himself after the fight. He had simply disappeared. Those who knew him at the Secret Service had now given up any hope that he could still be alive.

However, Bond was not dead; he had been captured by the Russians. They had taken him to a secret medical institute in Leningrad, where the KGB began trying to brainwash[8] him. After many months of torture[9], Bond had grown weaker and weaker and could take no more. The KGB had finally won their battle to control his mind.

A man called 'Colonel Boris' had then spent several more months carefully preparing Bond for his return to England. He had told Bond exactly how to behave, what to wear and even which hotel to stay in. He had also told him who to contact at the Secret Service Headquarters and precisely how to answer their many questions.

James Bond was sitting on his bed in The Ritz Hotel in London, holding the telephone to his ear. There was a moment of silence and then he heard a man's voice. 'This is Captain Walker speaking. Can I help you?'

9

Bond spoke slowly and clearly. 'This is Commander James Bond, agent number 007. Please would you put me through to M, or his secretary, Miss Moneypenny?'

Captain Walker was very surprised to hear what sounded like Bond's voice. He quickly pressed two buttons on the side of his phone. The first button started a machine which would record the conversation. The second sent a message to the Special Branch of the police, who would listen to the conversation, trace the call[10] and immediately arrange for the caller to be followed. Then Walker said, 'I'm afraid I don't know those two names. Who exactly are these people?'

'M is Admiral Sir Miles Messervy,' James Bond answered calmly. 'His office is on the eighth floor. He used to have a secretary called Miss Moneypenny. I want to see him.'

'No, I'm sorry,' Walker responded apologetically. 'I don't know either of them. Can you give me any more information?'

'Well, let's see what else I can tell you then ...' said Bond, frowning. 'It's Wednesday today. That means meat pie will be the main dish on the menu in the canteen.' Due to the brainwashing Bond could not remember all these things himself. He was using the detailed information that Colonel Boris had given him over the last few months.

Captain Walker thought for a moment. Could this man really be James Bond? There was always something strange about 007's death. They had never found a body. There was no solid evidence for his death. Perhaps he *had* escaped alive ... Walker decided to send him to the Security section of the Secret Service for further questioning.

'I'm afraid I can't help you myself,' he told Bond. 'But try Major Townsend. His office is at 44 Kensington Cloisters. I'll call and make an appointment for you to see him today.'

––––

A short while later James Bond left his hotel room, stepped out into a cold, clear November morning and got into a taxi. His every move was now being carefully watched by Special Branch police officers and a black car followed close behind his taxi.

'I'm here to see Major Townsend,' Bond announced when he arrived at Kensington Cloisters.

'Yes, he's expecting you, sir,' confirmed the man who had opened the door. 'Please come in. Shall I take your raincoat?'

The doorman put the coat on a hook near the entrance. As soon as he was inside Major Townsend's office, Bond's raincoat would be taken quickly upstairs to a laboratory[11]. There someone would test the material to find out where the coat had come from and if it really belonged to James Bond.

And now, as Bond followed the man down a long corridor, a hidden X-ray camera secretly took a picture of Bond and what he was carrying in his pockets. The man knocked on a door, opened it and asked Bond to go inside. It was a pleasant, very light room with expensive furniture.

A tall man with a friendly face stood up from a comfortable-looking chair, smiled and walked towards Bond. 'Come in and sit down,' he said warmly. 'Would you like a cigarette? I'm sorry, these aren't the ones I remember you prefer.' The man watched Bond carefully and noted his reaction.

Bond took a cigarette with a blank expression on his face and said nothing. Then both men sat down. Major Townsend crossed his legs comfortably. Bond sat up straight.

'Well, now. How can I help you?' enquired Townsend.

Bond looked at Major Townsend. Colonel Boris's description was very good – the big, friendly face, the brown eyes, the military moustache and the smart suit. But he had not mentioned how very cold and intelligent the eyes were.

'It's really quite simple,' Bond explained steadily. 'I am who I say I am. And I want to speak to M.'

'Yes,' replied Townsend, 'but you haven't been in contact with us for nearly a year. We all thought you were dead, so you'll understand that we must make sure that you really are 007.'

Major Townsend asked him several questions, which Bond answered fully and calmly. Then Townsend said, 'Now, please tell me where you've come from and where you've been all these months.'

'I'm sorry,' Bond apologized, 'but I can only tell that to M himself.'

'I see,' replied Major Townsend. He thought for a few seconds and then went on. 'Well, I'll make a telephone call and see what I can do. I'll only be a few minutes.' He stood up and picked up a newspaper from a nearby table. 'Would you like to see today's *Times*?' he asked, and held out the paper. Bond took it from him. His fingerprints were now on the specially treated newspaper, which would be carefully examined later.

Major Townsend went to the next room, closed the door, quickly telephoned the laboratory and then telephoned Bill Tanner, the Chief of Staff at the Secret Service Headquarters. 'Yes, sir,' he said a few moments later, 'I think it must be 007. He's wearing the same type of clothes he usually wears, although everything looks very new. The laboratory report says that his coat was bought yesterday in London. He answered all the questions correctly, but he's insisting that he'll only talk to M about what's happened. But I don't like it – he has a strange look in his eyes. I apologized for not being able to offer him his favourite type of cigarette, but he didn't know what I was talking about. And the X-ray camera showed that he's carrying a gun – a strange sort of weapon we haven't seen before. Personally, I don't think M should see him alone, although I think that's the only way we'll get him to talk to us.'

When Major Townsend went back into the other room a few minutes later, Bond was still sitting stiffly in the same chair. He was holding the newspaper but he had not opened it. Major Townsend smiled.

'Well, I've arranged everything,' he announced cheerfully. 'M is extremely pleased to hear that you are all right, and he'll be free to see you in about half an hour. A car should be here to collect you in about ten minutes and drive you there.'

James Bond smiled for the first time. But it was a thin smile, which did not light up his eyes.

2

The Attack

Bill Tanner, the Chief of Staff at the Secret Service, stood in front of M's desk. 'I really don't think you should see him on your own, sir,' he repeated firmly. 'There's no doubt that it's James – we've matched the fingerprints. But I don't like the feel of this at all. Why has he got new clothes? And why did he check into The Ritz and phone our main reception desk? He could have just phoned me on my personal number or come straight here to see you. It seems like a typical KGB brainwashing job to me.'

M looked up at Bill Tanner's tired, worried face and smiled. 'Thank you,' he said quietly, 'but I need to talk to 007 myself. When I sent him to Japan I had no idea that what should have been a peaceful job was going to end so badly. Or that 007 would go missing for a year. He's quite right. It was I who sent him on the mission and he has every right to report back to me personally. I'll see him, but I want you to wait in the next room and listen in to the conversation. And don't worry about his gun – I can use the new safety device[12].' M pointed up at a thin line on the ceiling. 'Are you sure that the glass wall will come down quickly enough when I press the button?' he asked.

'Yes, sir,' said the Chief of Staff nervously. 'We've tested it and it works all right. But …'

A light started to flash on M's intercom[13]. 'That must mean Bond is here,' said M. 'Tell him to come straight in, please.'

'Yes, sir,' Bill Tanner replied. Then he left the room and closed the door behind him.

James Bond was standing outside M's office. He was smiling strangely at Miss Moneypenny, who was sitting behind her desk and looking very upset, clearly confused by his odd behaviour. Then he turned and greeted the Chief of Staff flatly: 'Hello, Bill.'

'Hello, James,' responded Bill. 'Long time no see[P]. M is ready for you now, so let's talk when you come out.'

'That will be fine,' said Bond slowly. Then he went into M's office.

Bill walked quickly into the office next to M's and shut the door. He pressed a button on his desk. There was a small click, and then the sound of M's voice came into the room over a loud speaker. The Chief of Staff listened to what was being said in the next room. 'Hello, James. It's wonderful to see you again. Sit down and tell me all about it,' said M.

James Bond sat down in front of M. Bond knew this chair and had sat in it and talked to M many times before. Suddenly, lots of different, confused memories came quickly into his head. Bond tried not to think about them. He knew that he must think only about what he needed to say and do.

'I'm afraid I still can't remember very much, sir,' he said. 'I was hit on the head while I was doing that job in Japan. I was badly hurt and I lost my memory. To begin with I couldn't even remember who or where I was. The Russian police found me some months later in Vladivostok. I've no idea how I got there. The police passed me on to the KGB and when they checked my fingerprints they got very excited. For weeks they asked me question after question. I couldn't remember much but I told them what I could.'

'You told them what you could?' repeated M slowly. 'Was that a good idea?'

'They were very nice to me,' Bond replied. 'So I wanted to help them. Then I was taken to a hospital in Leningrad. While I was there specialist brain doctors came to look at my head. And other people came to talk to me about the political situation and that sort of thing. They explained to me how the East and West need to work together, for world peace. I hadn't thought about it in that way before and I think they are right.' He looked confidently across the table at M. 'However, you probably don't understand. You're always making war against someone. And you've been using me as a weapon to do that for you. But not anymore – that's finished.'

'You say the Russians want peace,' began M angrily. 'Then why do they need the KGB? At the last estimate, the KGB had about one hundred thousand men and women "making war", as you call it, against other countries. And did they tell you that they killed two of our agents in Munich last month?'

'Oh yes, sir,' Bond said in a patient voice. 'They have to protect themselves from the secret services of the West. But if you close down the British Secret Service, they won't need the KGB.'

'I don't believe that for one minute,' replied M shortly. 'Anyway, if the Russians are such good people, then why didn't you stay in their country?'

'We thought that it was more important for me to come back and fight for peace here, sir,' explained Bond. M noticed his use of the word 'we'. Just then Bond's right hand started to move slowly towards the pocket of his coat. M knew now that Bond was planning to kill him. He pushed his chair back from the desk and put his fingers on a button under the left arm of his chair.

Bond's face was white and he looked uncomfortable. He was staring at M and began to speak in a hard, forceful voice. 'We want to remove the people who are responsible for this war,' he said. 'And you are the first person on the list.'

Bond pulled his hand out of his coat pocket. He was holding a gun and was starting to point it towards M. M quickly pressed the button on the arm of his chair. With a loud rush of air, a large sheet of thick, bulletproof[14] glass dropped down in front of him from the ceiling. At the same moment brown, liquid poison[15] came from the gun and splashed onto the glass wall that now separated the two men.

Almost instantly Bill Tanner and another man came running into the room and threw themselves on James Bond. As they caught him his head fell forwards and his eyes closed. 'It's cyanide!' said Bill. 'He must have breathed some of the fumes in. We must all get out of here.' The men pulled Bond quickly from the room and M followed them.

'Don't tell anyone about this,' M said to the Chief of Staff a few minutes later. 'I'll call Sir James Molony at the Park Hospital and tell him what has happened. Take 007 down there – they'll know how to treat him. You heard Bond say what happened to him: he was hurt and as a result he lost his memory and then the KGB got him. They brainwashed him. All right? That's all.'

Bill Tanner was busy writing everything down in his notebook. But now he looked up. 'Don't you want to press any charges[P], sir? He tried to kill you,' he said.

'Certainly not,' answered M. '007 is a sick man and doesn't know what he's doing. Sir James knows about brainwashing and will know what to do. If the KGB has the nerve[P] to use one of my best men to attack me, then I have the nerve to send him back to attack them. 007 was a good agent once and I'm sure he'll be a good agent again. After lunch, please give me the information we have on Scaramanga. When 007 is ready, that will be his next mission.'

'Scaramanga!' the shocked Chief of Staff cried. 'But 007 wouldn't be able to kill him! No one can kill Scaramanga!'

'For what he tried to do here this morning,' said M coldly, '007 would have to spend twenty years or more in prison. I don't want that. It would be better for him to die on a mission. It will be a test. If he can kill Scaramanga, then we can forget the past. That's my final decision.'

At the same moment brown, liquid poison came from the gun and splashed onto the glass wall that now separated the two men.

3

Scaramanga

When M returned from lunch, he found Miss Moneypenny typing at her desk.

'Your office is safe to use again,' she informed him, 'but keep the windows open for a while. Oh, and here's the file you wanted, sir.'

M took the brown file from his secretary. It had a red 'Top Secret' star stamped on the top right-hand corner. 'How's 007? Did he wake up all right?' he enquired, concerned.

'I think so, sir,' replied Miss Moneypenny. 'The medical officer gave him a sedative[16] and then he was carried out of the back door under a blanket. No one's asked me any questions about it.'

'Good,' remarked M. He walked through the door into his office and sat down behind the large desk. For the hundredth time he assured himself that his decision was the right one. M opened the brown folder and started to read the report.

FRANCISCO SCARAMANGA

- Scaramanga is an assassin[17] who works mainly for the KGB in Havana, Cuba, and for other organizations in the Caribbean and Central American states.
- He is known to be responsible for the death of five British secret agents and has seriously injured another.
- He is well known in the Caribbean and is widely feared by the local people.
- He always uses a Colt .45 handgun made of gold and has therefore become known as 'The Man with the Golden Gun'. He uses gold and silver bullets, which are specially designed to cause maximum damage.
- The police are aware of him, although he has never been arrested.

DESCRIPTION
Age: about 35
Height: 1.9m
Eyes: light brown
Hair: short, red hair with a small moustache
Build: slim, strong, broad shoulders
Personality: ruthless[18], serious, enjoys the company of women

ORIGINS

- In his early years he lived in Spain and travelled with his father's circus. He learnt to use pistols very skilfully as part of his circus act. His childhood was difficult and painful.
- Aged 16 he shot a policeman during an incident at the circus. He then hid on a ship and travelled to America.
- On arrival in the United States he worked as a gunman for the 'Spangled Mob' in a Las Vegas hotel. His job was to execute people who had cheated at the casino.
- In 1958 he got into trouble with a rival[19] gang – the Purple Gang – and had to leave the United States. He then became rich by buying and selling property for criminals in the Caribbean.
- In 1959 he moved to Havana. When Fidel Castro came to power there after the revolution, Scaramanga began working for the Cuban Secret Police.

CONCLUSION

Scaramanga is a very cold, secretive paid assassin, with connections to the KGB and the Cuban Secret Police. A highly experienced and well-trained agent would be needed for this dangerous mission. However, the recommendation is that Scaramanga should be removed as soon as possible.

19

At the end of the report was a handwritten note, which read, 'I am in agreement,' and below it was the signature of the Head of the Caribbean and Central American Section. Next to this was the Chief of Staff's signature.

M looked up from the paper. For about five minutes he sat and gazed across the room. Then he reached for his pen and wrote the word, 'Action?' and signed the page.

He sat very still for another five minutes and wondered whether he had just signed James Bond's death warrant[P].

4

To Jamaica

It was a hot, oppressive day when James Bond's flight arrived in Jamaica. Several months had passed since the terrible incident in M's office and, following Bond's intensive and difficult rehabilitation at the Park Hospital in London, he had been declared fit enough to be sent on a new mission.

For six weeks now Bond had been travelling around the Caribbean and Central America trying to track down his target – Scaramanga. He had apparently missed him by just one day in Caracas. But now he had lost the trail. He was waiting in Kingston International Airport for a flight to Havana as Scaramanga was known to have spent a lot of time in Cuba. It seemed too obvious to search there, but Bond was running out of places to look.

Bond wandered around the airport looking at the shops to kill time[P]. As he did so he walked past a notice board, which held messages for passengers travelling through the airport. He stopped and looked to see if there were any messages under the letter 'H' for 'Hazard, Mark' – the false name that he was travelling under. Nothing. He was not surprised – in all his life he had never found a message for him at an airport. But then, as he walked past 'S', he suddenly froze. He looked around, as casually as possible, to make sure no one was watching him. Then he covered his hand with his handkerchief and quickly reached out and took an envelope on which was written the word 'Scaramanga'. A few moments later, Bond walked calmly to the nearby men's toilets and, when he was safely inside, he carefully opened the envelope. The message he found read:

To: Scaramanga, BOAC passenger from Lima, Peru
From:

MESSAGE
Message received from Kingston, Jamaica, at 12.15: 3½ Beckford, SLM, from midday tomorrow.

Bond could not believe his eyes[P]. At last he had some solid information! Bond read the message again and then carefully slid the piece of paper back into the envelope and returned it to the notice board. Then he found the British Overseas Airways Corporation desk and checked their flight timetables. Yes, the BOAC flight from Lima to Kingston was due in at 13.15 the next day.

Bond thought quickly about what he needed to do. He walked to the Cuban Airlines desk and cancelled his flight reservation to Havana, before finding a public telephone and calling the Head of the British Secret Service in Jamaica. After a moment he heard a girl's voice on the line. 'Commander Ross's secretary speaking. Can I help you?'

'Could you put me through to Commander Ross, please?' asked Bond. 'This is a friend of his from London.'

'I'm afraid Commander Ross is away from Jamaica,' replied the girl. Bond thought her voice sounded a little familiar. 'Is there anything I can do?' she offered brightly.

'Well, my name's …' started Bond.

'Don't tell me,' the girl said excitedly. 'It's James, isn't it?'

Bond laughed. It was his wonderful secretary from the old days in the Double-0 section. 'Mary Goodnight!' he exclaimed. 'What on earth^P are you doing here?'

'More or less the same job that I used to do for you,' she answered warmly. 'I was so pleased to hear you were back, but I thought you were ill or something. How wonderful to hear from you! Where are you now?'

'Kingston Airport,' said Bond. 'Now listen, Mary. I need your help and quickly. We can talk later. First, do the initials SLM mean anything to you?'

'No, I don't think so,' she said slowly. 'Oh, I'm not sure, but they could stand for Savanna-La-Mar. That's a town in the south of the island.'

Bond spoke decisively. 'Right. I need a car, any car. And a detailed map of Jamaica. Can you bring the car to Morgan's Harbour? I'm going to stay there tonight.'

'All right,' replied Goodnight. 'Anything else?'

'Yes, wear something pretty and bring me one hundred pounds in Jamaican money so I can buy you dinner,' added Bond, smiling broadly to himself.

She laughed. 'Well, now I know it's definitely you, James! I'll see you at about seven.'

———

Bond was drinking a Bourbon whisky with ice when Mary Goodnight walked into the little bar on the waterfront later that evening. 'Oh, James!' she cried and kissed him on the cheek. 'It's so wonderful to have you back.' She was wearing a stylish, orangey-pink dress and a pearl necklace, and James thought that she looked beautiful.

'It's good to see you again,' Bond told her warmly. 'So, tell me the news. Have you managed to get what I asked for?'

She handed him an envelope, saying, 'Here's the money. And the car's outside – it's old, but the tank's full of petrol and it's reliable.'

While they ate dinner Mary Goodnight brought Bond up to date[P] with what was happening in Jamaica. 'There are a lot of problems with the sugar cane crops[20],' she explained. 'Sugar cane is worth a lot of money to Jamaica. Cuba's sugar crop is Jamaica's main rival, but with the recent hurricane and all the rain they've been having there, the Cuban crop is only going to be about three million tons this year – that's less than half of what it should be. So Castro wants to keep the world price high and sell as much Cuban sugar cane to Russia as possible. They say that he's actually paying people to burn the rival Jamaican crops so he can sell the Cuban sugar at a high price. And Savanna-La-Mar, those initials you were asking me about, that's the area where most of the Jamaican sugar cane crops are grown. WISCO – the West Indian Sugar Company – has a huge sugar-growing estate near there at Frome. The top man of the company, Tony Hugill, is having a lot of problems because his crops keep being burnt.'

They discussed the political situation in Jamaica for a few minutes and then Bond asked thoughtfully, 'And where's your chief, Commander Ross?'

'Well, I don't really know,' answered Goodnight in a worried tone. 'He went to Trinidad last week to look for somebody called Scaramanga – a local gunman of some sort. Commander Ross was due back two days ago, but he still hasn't turned up. I've informed Headquarters and they've told me to wait for another week.'

'I much prefer working with his assistant anyway,' remarked Bond with a smile.

5

Number 3½ Beckford Street

The next morning, having studied the map, James Bond got into the old car and began the 200-kilometre drive down to the south coast of the island. It was around midday when he finally arrived in the small, unattractive town of Savanna-La-Mar. He parked the car near the quiet seafront and wandered casually back into the streets of the town. Bond stopped and asked a shop owner if there was a road named 'Beckford' somewhere in the town. He was informed that there was a Beckford Street and was given directions to it. Bond walked on and, after several wrong turns, eventually found number 3½ Beckford Street. It was a big, wooden house with steps up to the front door and an old sign that read 'Dreamland Café'. Once, the building would have been quite grand, but now it looked tired and the paint was peeling off. In the front garden there was a large tree, covered in beautiful, blue flowers. In the welcoming shade of this tree, a young woman was sitting in a rocking chair reading a magazine.

Bond walked up the steps and through the open door into the café. He was looking at the various unappetizing plates of food on the counter when he heard quick footsteps outside. The girl from the garden came in and walked towards the counter. She was pretty with long, black hair and big, brown eyes.

She greeted him in a friendly voice, 'Afternoon'.

'Good afternoon,' replied Bond. 'Could I have a bottle of beer, please?'

'Sure.' She walked slowly behind the counter, opened a bottle and passed it to Bond together with a glass that was almost clean. 'That's one shilling[21] and sixpence.'

Bond paid for his beer and then pulled a stool up to the counter and sat down on it.

'Are you just here for the day?' the girl asked, as she leant on the counter.

'Yes, that's right,' he replied. 'My name's Mark.'

'And I'm Tiffy,' she replied.

'Do you own this place?' Bond asked her.

'No!' said the girl and laughed. 'I'm just the manager. It might be quiet now, but it's busy in the evenings.' She looked towards a clock on the wall – it was half-past one.

'Oh,' exclaimed the girl suddenly, 'I've forgotten to feed Joe and May.' She walked over to one of the windows and opened it. At once, from the direction of the large tree, two big black birds flew down and through the open window. They flew around the room and, with loud cries, landed untidily on the counter top within reach of Bond's hand. Tiffy broke a biscuit into small bits and held them for the birds, who greedily took the pieces from her fingers.

'They're called Jamaican grackles,' she explained, smiling. 'They're very friendly.'

She reached for another biscuit but then stopped, arm outstretched, and listened. The sound of footsteps came from upstairs and the smile fell from her face. 'There's a man upstairs who rents a room for meetings. He's an important man, but I don't like him. He's rough and he doesn't like Joe and May. He says they make too much noise.' She waved her arms, trying to get the birds to fly in the direction of the open window, but they wanted the second biscuit and refused to move. Tiffy turned to Bond and begged him urgently, 'Please, just sit quietly, whatever he says. He likes to make people angry and then …' Her face was suddenly very serious.

At that moment, a door opened behind the counter and a large man quietly stepped into the room. He came up and leant on the counter, without saying a word. The description of him in the report Bond had been given was exact, but he had not expected the man's shoulders to be so wide, or that there would

25

be no emotion in the small eyes that now examined Bond coldly. He was wearing an expensive-looking suit, a tie and a gold tie pin in the shape of a tiny pistol. There could be no doubt – this was Scaramanga.

Scaramanga looked towards the birds, then back at Bond and then said, 'I sometimes make them dance. Then I shoot their feet off.'

'Really?' replied Bond confidently. 'That sounds a bit extreme. What do you do it for?'

'The last time, it was for five thousand dollars. It seems like you don't know who I am. Didn't the girl tell you?'

Bond glanced towards Tiffy. She was standing very still and she looked nervous.

'Why should she?' Bond asked as he moved his hand ever so slightly nearer to the gun which was pushed into his waistband. 'Why would I want to know?'

Suddenly, there was flash of gold. 'Because of this,' replied Scaramanga aggressively as he pointed his gun at Bond's stomach. 'What are you doing here, stranger? We don't usually get tourists here. You're not from the police, are you? Or any of their friends?'

A second passed, then Bond casually crossed his legs and allowed a small smile to appear on his face. He turned to Tiffy and said, 'Well, I've no idea who this man is, but ask him what he'd like to drink. Whoever he is, that was a good circus act.'

Tiffy looked terrified and did not move. She opened her mouth to speak but no sound came out. Suddenly, the two birds, perhaps sensing the tension in the room, cried out and took off towards the open window, like two thieves escaping.

The shots from the gold Colt .45 handgun were deafening. The two birds exploded in mid air and black feathers flew in all directions. Then there was a moment of awful silence. James Bond did not move. Tiffy grabbed his bottle of beer from the counter and threw it angrily across the room, then she fell to the floor, crying loudly.

Bond picked up his glass and drank what was left of the beer, then he got slowly to his feet. He walked towards Scaramanga, looked him directly in the eyes and then walked past him over to where Tiffy was lying. He knelt down beside her and helped her to sit up. He then took a cloth, wetted it at the tap and gently wiped it over her face.

6

The Easy Grand

Once Tiffy had calmed down, Bond stood up and turned to face Scaramanga again.

'That may have been a good circus act, but it was rough on the girl. Give her some money,' Bond demanded. Knowing Scaramanga's history, Bond had used the word 'circus' again on purpose.

'No,' replied Scaramanga simply. Then, suspiciously, 'And what's all this talk of circuses? Like I said before, are you with the cops[22]? You certainly seem like you are.'

'People don't tell me what to do. I tell them,' stated Bond, then he walked into the middle of the room and sat down at a table. 'Stop trying to give me a hard time[P] and come and sit down,' he added.

Scaramanga's expression did not change. He slowly walked across the room, picked up one of the metal chairs, turned it around and sat down on it facing the wrong way round. His right hand rested on the top of his leg, centimetres away from the handle of his gun, which was tucked into the top of his trousers. Bond recognized that this was a sensible working position for a gunman – the metal back of the chair was in front of him protecting his body. This was certainly a most careful and professional man.

Bond, with both hands in full view on the table top, said in a relaxed way, 'No, I'm not from the police. My name's Mark Hazard. I'm from a company called Transworld Consortium. I've been doing a job at Frome, the WISCO sugar place. Do you know it?'

'Of course I know it. What have you been doing there?' asked Scaramanga.

'Not so fast, my friend. First of all, who are you and what's your business?' said Bond firmly.

'Scaramanga. Francisco Scaramanga. I work in labour relations[23]. "The Man with the Golden Gun" is what they call me around here,' he said coldly.

'Well,' said Bond, looking thoughtful, 'a gun can be a useful tool for solving labour problems. We could do with you[P] up at Frome.'

'Have they been having trouble up there?' Scaramanga asked, but he looked bored.

'Yes, they've been having too many sugar cane fires. One of the jobs of my company is insurance investigation[24],' lied Bond.

'Ah,' sneered Scaramanga, 'security work. I thought I could smell the cop-smell.' He looked satisfied that his guess had been close enough. 'Did you catch anyone?'

'Most of them,' explained Bond, 'but not all of them. That's why I say we could do with a good "labour relations" person up there.'

There was a pause and then Scaramanga asked Bond, 'Do you carry a gun?'

'Of course. You don't go after people like that without one.'

'What kind of gun?' Scaramanga wanted to know.

'A Walther PPK 7.65 millimetre,' said Bond.

Scaramanga seemed impressed by this and remained silent for a moment. Then he turned to Tiffy.

'Hey, two bottles of beer, if you're in business again.' He turned back and looked hard at Bond. 'What's your next job?'

'"The Man with the Golden Gun" is what they call me.'

'I don't know. I'm in no hurry. I'll call London and see if they've got any other problems in the area. I work for them more or less on a freelance[25] basis.'

Tiffy came out from behind the counter and brought the drinks to the table. She gave Scaramanga a long, hard look and then turned around sharply and walked away.

A few moments passed while both men simply sat and drank their beers. Scaramanga appeared to be deep in thought about something. At last he spoke. 'Do you want to earn yourself a grand – a thousand dollars?'

Bond said, 'Possibly.' Then after a moment he added, 'Probably.' But what he was really thinking was, 'Yes, definitely. If it means being able to stay near you.'

Scaramanga did not take his cold eyes from Bond's face. Now he began to talk more openly to Bond. 'I've got a problem, mister,' he began. 'Some partners of mine have taken an interest in the Negril property development. It's at a place called Bloody Bay – about thirty kilometres down the coast from here. Do you know it?'

Bond told the man that he had seen the area on the map, near Green Island Harbour.

'Right. Well I've got shares[26] in the business. We started building a hotel there, but halfway through building it, the tourist industry went quiet – the Americans probably got frightened of being so close to Cuba. And the banks have got difficult with us, so we've started to run out of money.'

'So you're trapped – you haven't got the money to finish it and presumably it's not easy to sell,' summarized Bond.

'Right. So I came here a few days ago and I'm staying at the Thunderbird Hotel – the one that we've only half finished. I've asked half a dozen[27] of the main shareholders to fly in for a meeting straight away, to decide what to do next. Now, I want to give these guys a good time, so I've arranged everything – a great night with a band from Kingston, singers, dancers. There's even a small railway near the hotel that used to transport the sugar cane. The next day I'll take them on a train trip down that line to Green Island Harbour where I've got a big, luxury motorboat. So they can go deep-sea fishing and have a really good time. Do you get me?^P'

Bond nodded. Scaramanga looked into Bond's eyes. 'Some of these men are sort of rough. We're all shareholders, but that doesn't mean we're friends. I want to hold some meetings, private meetings, with maybe only two or three guys at a time, to find out what all the different interests are. It could be that some of the other guys, the ones not invited to a particular meeting, might try to bug[28] a meeting, or try to find out in some other way what's been said. So ... it's just occurred to me that you could act as a kind of guard at those meetings. You would check the room for microphones, then stay outside the door and make sure that no one comes nosing around^P.'

Bond could not stop himself from laughing. Then he said, 'So you want to hire me as a kind of personal bodyguard. Is that right?'

Scaramanga frowned. 'And what's so funny about that, mister? It's good money, isn't it? Three, maybe four days in a luxury hotel like the Thunderbird, for a thousand dollars?' He stared at Bond.

Bond scratched the back of his head, thinking quickly. He knew he had not heard the full story. He also knew it was odd for this man to hire a complete stranger to do this job for him. However, it did make sense that Scaramanga would not want to hire a local man, an ex-policeman for example, even if he could find one – local people know too much. If Bond accepted the offer, it would be a perfect way to stay close to Scaramanga and find out more. Yet it felt too convenient to be true. Could it be a trap? Bond decided to take the risk.

He then said, 'I was only laughing at the idea of a man like you wanting protection. But it all sounds great fun. Of course I'll come along. When do we start?'

7

Into Scaramanga's World

It was early evening now and Bond was driving his car, in the dark, along a country road he did not know. He had been told to follow Scaramanga's car to get to the half-built Thunderbird Hotel. He knew more or less the direction they were travelling in and could tell that the sea had always been close to him on his left while he had been driving, but he felt uncomfortable. The first law for a secret agent is to be sure of exactly where he is, to know his route of escape and to have a means of communication with the outside world. For the last hour, James Bond had been driving into the unknown, and his nearest contact was a girl he hardly knew in a bar thirty kilometres away. The situation was worrying.

Just as Bond was considering his position, some glowing lights appeared up ahead and what had to be the hotel began to sweep into view. The two cars came to a stop in front of the building. With the darkness of the night hiding the evidence of any building work, the brilliantly lit entrance to the hotel looked impressive and convincing enough. James Bond got out of his car and followed Scaramanga inside, where a hotel clerk, dressed in a smart uniform, came to greet them. Bond wrote 'Mark Hazard' and the London address of Transworld Consortium in the hotel register.

After speaking for several moments to the hotel manager, Scaramanga turned to Bond and said, 'You're in room number 24, in the west wing. I'm close by in number 20. Order whatever you want from Room Service. See you at about ten o'clock in the morning. The guys will be coming in from Kingston at around midday. OK?' The expressionless face and cold eyes did not care if it was OK or not. Bond said it was.

———

Once inside the pleasant, modern, double bedroom, Bond turned off the air conditioning – he had never liked the idea of it – and opened the window. Then he inspected the room in detail. He checked behind the paintings on the walls and under the bed, and then he slowly unscrewed the bottom plate of the telephone. As he suspected, he discovered a small microphone, which had been connected to the main cable inside. He smiled to himself, left the microphone untouched and then carefully replaced the bottom plate and put the phone back on the bedside table. He knew this kind of device well. It would be powerful enough to pick up and transmit a conversation from anywhere in the room.

James Bond unpacked his few belongings and then called Room Service and ordered some food. While he was waiting for his food to arrive, he poured himself a glass of whisky and sat down near the open window. He could hear the waves breaking softly on the nearby beach and could smell the sea air. As he sat holding the glass of whisky in one hand, he thought about what would happen the next day. It would certainly be interesting to see these fat, frightened shareholders! Bond had a strong suspicion that they would be gangsters – the type of men who owned the Havana hotels and discos, or who were in control in Las Vegas and Miami. And who was Scaramanga working for – whose money was he representing? It could be anyone in the Caribbean, yet Bond was sure that the money would have come from criminal sources. He was probably still working for the Cuban Secret Police. And what about the man himself? The incident with the birds certainly proved that Scaramanga knew what he was doing with a gun. How on earth was Bond going to kill him?

Later, after eating dinner in his room, Bond pushed his empty suitcase up against the bedroom door and balanced three empty glasses on top of it. Although only a simple booby trap[29], it would give him all the warning he needed if anyone tried to come into his room. Then he undressed, got into bed and slept.

———

After a night full of disturbing dreams, James Bond woke up at half-past seven. He got dressed, had a quick breakfast in his room and then decided to go for a walk to find out more about the property. It did not take long to get a good picture of[P] the place. The darkness of the night before had covered up a half-project. Bond now clearly saw that the east wing of the hotel had only just been started, while in the main section of the building there were workmen everywhere. They were hurriedly fitting carpets, hanging curtains and even painting walls. But no one was employed on the essentials – the big cement mixers and diggers lay untouched outside. Beyond the newly laid gardens, the wild mangrove swamps[30] spread out far and wide, full of crocodiles and giving off a strong, unpleasant smell.

Bond guessed that the place needed at least another year and another five million dollars before it would be properly finished. Some of the shareholders were not going to be happy when they saw this; they might want to sell their shares in it. But other businessmen might want to buy into it, as long as they could do so cheaply, and use it as a tax-loss to set against more profitable business elsewhere. Businessmen often preferred to have money in property here because Jamaica gave big tax concessions[31] – that was better than having to pay high taxes to the government in the United States, Cuba or anywhere else. So, Scaramanga planned to blind his guests with pleasure and send them back happy to their syndicates[32], so that they would recommend buying into the project. Would it work? Bond seriously doubted it.

Bond glanced at his watch. It was nearly ten o'clock, so he walked back to the main reception desk of the hotel. Scaramanga, dressed in another smart suit, was at the desk talking to the manager. He nodded to Bond. 'Let's go and have a look at the conference room,' he said.

Bond followed him through the hotel bar to a big, simply furnished room. It had a large, round table with a telephone on it and seven white leather chairs around it. Bond began to look carefully around the room. He said, 'The wall lights could be bugged. And, of course, the telephone. Do you want me to have a close look at it?'

Scaramanga turned to Bond and answered, 'There's no need to. It's definitely bugged. By me. I've got to have a record of exactly what is said.'

'All right, then. Where do you want me to be?' Bond asked.

'Sit outside the door,' Scaramanga told him. 'Read a magazine or something. There'll be a general meeting this afternoon at around four. Tomorrow there'll be one or two smaller meetings. I want all these meetings to be private. I don't want anyone to disturb us.'

'No problem,' replied Bond confidently. 'Now, isn't it time you told me the names of these men, who they represent and which ones, if any, you're expecting trouble from?'

Scaramanga picked up a pad of paper and a pencil from the table and handed them to Bond. 'Sit down, then. First, there's Mr Hendriks. He's a Dutchman and he represents the European money – mostly Swiss. He's not the arguing type so he should be OK. Then there's Sam Binion from Detroit. He and his friends are worth about twenty million dollars. Next there's Leroy Gengerella. Miami. He's big in the entertainment world and owns Gengerella Enterprises. He's the kind of person who wants quick profits – he might be rough. And Ruby Rotkopf, the hotel man from Las Vegas. He'll ask the most difficult questions because he'll already know most of the answers from experience. Hal Garfinkel from Chicago. He's in labour relations, like me, and represents a lot of Teamster Union funds. He shouldn't be any trouble. That makes five so far. The last one is Louie Paradise from Phoenix, Arizona. He's involved in casinos and owns Paradise Slots – the biggest company in the one-armed bandit[33] business. I'm not sure what he's going to say.'

'And who do you represent, Mr Scaramanga?' asked Bond casually.

35

'Caribbean money,' came the vague reply.

'Cuban?' said Bond, pushing him further.

'I said Caribbean. Cuba's in the Caribbean, isn't it?'

'Castro or Batista?' insisted Bond.

A heavy frown fell on Scaramanga's face and his right hand formed into a fist. 'Stay out of my business, mister,' he warned, 'or you'll get hurt. And I mean that.' Then he turned and walked quickly out of the room.

James Bond smiled. He looked down at the list of names in front of him. It certainly looked like a suspicious group of men. But the name he was most interested in was Mr Hendriks, who represented 'European money'. Bond felt sure that this man was probably not what he seemed.

Bond picked up the pad of paper and walked back to the hotel reception area. A large man was approaching the desk from the entrance. He looked hot and uncomfortable in his formal suit. He looked like a typical European businessman – a German dentist or a Swiss banker. He put down his heavy suitcase next to the reception desk and said in a heavy European accent and with poor English grammar, 'It is Mr Hendriks. I think it is that you are having a room for me, isn't it?'

8

The Six Men

The men on the list had begun to arrive. Scaramanga was there in the hotel lobby to greet them and Bond stood nearby, mentally trying to match each man to one of the names on the list as they came through the door. They all looked quite similar – dark-faced, clean-shaven, hard eyes – and each one carried a briefcase. Bond also noticed that one or two of them were carrying guns under their suit jackets. Once they had all arrived, Scaramanga walked over to Bond and told him, 'See you in the bar around twelve o'clock. I'll be introducing you as my personal assistant.'

Bond nodded before strolling off in the direction of his bedroom. When he walked into the room he carefully checked that everything was exactly as it had been when he had left the room at about nine o'clock that morning. His razor was a couple of millimetres closer to the basin than it had been before. He now knew without question that his room had been searched while he was out and that a real expert had done it.

Bond was pleased. It was good to know that at last the fight really had begun. He took a shower and afterwards he looked at himself in the bathroom mirror and smiled. At last, after so many difficult months, he saw the real James Bond looking back at him. He felt a wave of excitement pass through him. He was ready for this mission.

———

When Bond walked into the bar just an hour or so later, all the men were already there, wearing more relaxed clothes and drinking champagne. Scaramanga stood leaning against the bar and was spinning his golden gun round and round on the first finger of his right hand like a character from an old Western film. As the door closed with a 'click' behind Bond, Scaramanga swung round and the golden gun suddenly stopped in mid turn, its barrel pointing directly at Bond's stomach.

'Guys,' said Scaramanga loudly, 'meet my personal assistant, Mr Mark Hazard, from London, England. He's come along to make sure things run smoothly this weekend. Mark, come here and meet everyone.' He lowered the gun and pushed it into the top of his trousers.

Bond, knowing that this was his chance to get to know more about the men, smiled and walked up to the bar. He ordered a gin and began to move among the gangsters, making small talk[P].

With one man he asked how his flight had been, with another he enquired about the weather in the United States and commented on the beautiful scenery in Jamaica. As he talked to each man he made a mental note of his voice and recalled his name. After a while, Bond walked purposefully towards Mr Hendriks and tried to start a conversation. 'It seems we're the only two Europeans here. I gather you're from Holland. I've often passed through it, but never stayed there. It's a beautiful country,' commented Bond.

'Yes,' answered Hendriks simply and with a heavy accent.

'What part do you come from?' Bond enquired.

'Den Haag,' came the short reply.

'Have you lived there long?' asked Bond.

'Many years,' replied Hendriks.

'It's a very beautiful town,' said Bond.

'Yes,' said Hendriks without interest. Bond waited a moment to see if he would add anything further, but nothing happened.

'Is this your first visit to Jamaica?' asked Bond, hoping to get more than one word in reply.

'No,' replied the Dutchman, and he looked straight past Bond in the direction of the bar. 'Excuse me, please,' he added drily and then moved away. He walked over to Scaramanga, who was standing alone leaning against the bar. Mr Hendriks said something and his words acted like a command on the other man. Mr Scaramanga stood up straight and immediately followed Mr Hendriks into a far corner of the room. Then he stood and listened carefully as Mr Hendriks talked rapidly in a low voice.

Bond watched the scene closely. He noted with interest the way in which Scaramanga, who until now had been full of arrogance and self-importance, treated this man with respect and deference. Seeing Mr Hendriks now, Bond guessed that he must be part of either the Mafia[34] or the KGB.

After having lunch together, the group of men split up and went to their rooms to rest for a few hours before the conference started.

Later that afternoon, as Bond returned from his room and walked through the lobby, the hotel manager came out from behind the reception desk. 'Er, Mr Hazard?'

'Yes,' answered Bond.

'I don't think you've met my assistant manager, Mr Travis,' he stated.

'No, I don't think I have,' said Bond.

'Would you like to step into my office for a moment and meet him?' he asked politely.

'Later perhaps. I'm on my way to the conference,' Bond explained.

The smartly dressed man came a step closer, then said quietly, 'He particularly wants to meet you, Mr – er – Bond.'

Bond suddenly understood. This man was clearly also working undercover[35], like him, and possibly wanted to introduce him to another agent. 'Right,' agreed Bond. 'We'd better make it quick.'

The manager stepped behind the desk and opened a door. Bond went in and the manager closed the door behind them. A tall, slim man was standing with his back to them leaning over a desk. He turned. He had straight, fair hair, a bronzed Texan face and instead of a right hand he had a bright, metal hook. Bond stopped in his tracks[P]. A broad smile spread across his face and his eyes shone with joy. 'Felix Leiter! I can't believe it's you!' he cried and went up to the man and gave him a friendly punch on the shoulder.

The face was slightly more lined than Bond remembered, but the man's smile was just as friendly and warm as it had always been. The men knew each other well – Leiter was in the CIA[36] and had worked with Bond on several previous missions. They had been through a lot together and during one very challenging mission, several years earlier, Leiter had lost his right arm and part of his left leg to a shark. Bond was hugely relieved[37] to know that Leiter was also 'working' for Scaramanga, and that he would no longer be working on this mission alone.

9

The Conference

James Bond left the reception area and quickly made his way to the bar. When he got there he saw that all the men were already seated around the table in the adjacent conference room and that Scaramanga was waiting impatiently by the door. 'Right,' he said, looking directly into Bond's eyes. 'Lock the door and wait outside while we're talking. Don't let anyone in, not even if the hotel catches fire.' And with that he turned and went inside to join the other six men.

Bond looked into the room and noted the seating order before he closed and locked the door as he had been told to do. He then quickly locked the other door, which led from the bar into the hotel lobby. Moving quietly and rapidly, he picked up a champagne glass from the bar and placed the bowl of the glass against the conference room door. Holding the glass by the stem, he placed his left ear against its base and listened. What had been the unintelligible rumble of a voice now became Mr Hendriks speaking: '... and I have a very important message for our Chairman from my superiors in Europe. It is from a sure source. There is a man called James Bond who is looking for him here. This is a man who is from the British Secret Service. I have no information or description of this man, but my superiors believe that he is a serious threat. Mr Scaramanga, have you heard of him?'

Scaramanga laughed loudly, 'No, I haven't! And should I care? I eat one of their famous secret agents for breakfast from time to time. Only ten days ago, I killed one of them who came looking for me. A man called Ross. His body is now very slowly sinking to the bottom of an oil lake in Trinidad. Next question, please, Mr Hendriks.'

'We must talk about the cane sabotage[38],' began Hendriks. 'At our meeting six months ago in Havana it was decided to help Fidel Castro to maintain, and even increase, the world price of sugar to balance out the damage caused by hurricane Flora. Our help would be in exchange for certain favours from him. This decision was taken against my wishes. Since that time there have been a lot of fires in the sugar cane fields of Jamaica and Trinidad. And my superiors have discovered that some members of this group – Mr Gengerella, Mr Rotkopf, Mr Binion and indeed our Chairman – have been purchasing large quantities of July sugar futures[39] in order to make money for themselves.'

There came low, angry voices from around the table. 'Why shouldn't we?' shouted Gengerella. 'Who said we weren't allowed to make money? Isn't that one of the reasons we are all here? I asked you six months ago, Mr Hendriks, and I'll ask you again now, which of your "superiors" wants to keep the price of raw sugar down? My guess is that it's Soviet Russia. They're selling goods to Cuba – including a recent shipment of missiles to fire against the United States, my homeland – in exchange for raw sugar. Mr Hendriks, is one of your "superiors" somebody in the Kremlin?'

The voice of Scaramanga shouted for calm and a reluctant silence fell. 'When we formed this group, we all agreed to work together,' Scaramanga reminded the men. 'So, Mr Hendriks, let me explain. As an investment group, we have good bets and bad bets. Sugar is a good bet and we should continue to bet on it even if you personally have decided not to be involved in it. Now listen. At this moment there are six ships controlled by this group that are waiting outside New York and other US harbours. These ships are loaded with raw sugar. These ships, Mr Hendriks, will not dock and unload their sugar until sugar futures, July futures specifically, have risen by another ten cents. The US government, the sugar lobby[40] and other powerful groups know this. They know that we have them cornered[P]. They want the ships to dock and the sugar to be unloaded before there's a real shortage and the price rises too high. But there's another side to it. It's costing us a lot of money to have our ships sitting there, waiting. So the situation can't carry on like this forever. One side will win, and one side will lose. Four of us here could win or lose about ten million dollars. And at the same time our investment in this Thunderbird Hotel isn't looking good – it's in the red[P]. So what do you think, Mr Hendriks? Of course we burn the sugar crops if we can get away with it. I know the right people in Jamaica and I pay them to do the job for us. That's how it works. So you just tell your superiors that what goes up must come down. And that's true for the price of sugar, like anything else. OK?'

There was a moment of silence before Mr Hendriks spoke.

'I will pass on what you say. But they will not be happy.' Then he added, 'Now there is the question of this hotel. What is the exact financial situation? I think we all want to know the truth.'

There was a murmur of agreement around the table and then Scaramanga began a long and detailed explanation, which was of little interest to Bond. In any case, Felix Leiter had told him that the whole meeting would be secretly recorded on electronic equipment in the small room where they had seen each other earlier. Leiter was working with the smart American hotel manager – an undercover electronics expert in the CIA, whose real name was Nick Nicholson – and their job was to get a better understanding of the members of the group and what they were trying to do. Leiter had confirmed what Bond had suspected: Hendriks was in fact a top man in the KGB. The CIA believed that Gengerella was a member of the Mafia. This was therefore a worrying situation, the first time that a Mafia member had been found working with the KGB, and it would need to be ended, Leiter said, by 'removing' someone if necessary.

Bond had explained his own mission to Leiter and Nicholson, and they had agreed that they should continue to work separately, but they would support each other if the need arose. So now Bond was on his own outside the conference room and Scaramanga was just finishing what he was saying. 'So in summary, gentlemen, we need to find another ten million dollars. The interests that I represent, which are the majority of the interests, believe that a loan[41] for this amount of money should be provided to the project by all of us. We would be paid interest at a rate of ten per cent and the loan would be repayable in ten years.'

The voice of Mr Rotkopf broke in angrily. 'Not on your life![P] What about the seven per cent second mortgage[42] my friends and I agreed to only a year ago? If I went back to Las Vegas and told them about this new loan, what do you think they would do to me?'

'We don't have a choice. It's that or the hotel closes,' responded Scaramanga calmly. 'What do you other guys say?'

Hendriks said, 'Ten per cent is a very good rate. My friends and I will lend one million dollars, as long as the agreement is clear and fair.'

'OK, OK,' Mr Binion murmured reluctantly. 'Count us in for the same amount. But this had better be the last time!'

In turn, the other men all agreed to lend a share of the money, although Mr Rotkopf was still unhappy. 'No, I don't want any part of this,' he said firmly. 'As soon as I get back I'm going to find the best lawyers in the States. You can't just cancel that mortgage!'

There was silence. The voice of Scaramanga was soft and deadly. 'You're making a big mistake. This is a nice, big tax-loss to balance out your Las Vegas business interests. And don't forget that we all promised each other that we would work together. Are you sure your answer is no?'

'I am absolutely sure,' he stated decisively.

'Would this help to change your mind?' Scaramanga said coldly. There was a loud gunshot and a sudden scream of terror. Something – possibly a chair – fell to the floor with a crash and then there was silence. Then someone coughed nervously and Mr Gengerella said calmly, 'I think that was the right solution to an embarrassing difference of opinion. Mr Rotkopf's friends in Las Vegas like a quiet life – I'm sure they won't even complain. Let's say that he has agreed that he and his friends will put in a million dollars, shall we?'

'Yes, that's right,' came Scaramanga's voice, happy and relaxed. 'Mr Rotkopf has left here to go back to Las Vegas. We never saw him again. We don't know anything, do we? I've got some hungry crocodiles out there in the swamps that need feeding. There'll be nothing left of poor Mr Rotkopf after they've had their dinner. I'll need some help with it tonight, though. Can you come with me, Gengerella? And you, Paradise?'

'No, not me!' pleaded the voice of Mr Paradise. 'It's against my religion.'

Mr Hendriks said, 'I will take his place. I am not a religious person.'

'Fine,' said Scaramanga and added, 'Well, guys, is there any other business to discuss? If not, we'll finish the meeting and have a drink.'

Hal Garfinkel broke in nervously, 'Just a minute. What about that British guy outside the door? He must have heard the gunshot. What's he going to say about it?'

Mr Scaramanga's laugh was dry and cruel. 'Don't worry about him. I picked him up in a bar a few kilometres away. I've only got temporary staff here to make sure you guys have a good time this weekend – and he's the most temporary of all of them. Those crocodiles really are hungry. Rotkopf will be the main course, but they'll need a dessert. For all I know he might be this James Bond man Mr Hendriks has told us about. No, don't you worry about the British guy. I'll sort him out.'

Bond carried the empty champagne glass over to the bar and slowly filled it with champagne. At that moment he heard Scaramanga turning his key in the lock. Scaramanga looked at Bond from the doorway. 'OK, that's enough champagne. Go to the manager and tell him Mr Rotkopf will be checking out tonight. And say that a major fuse[43] blew during the meeting and no one can go into this room and that I'm going to find out why we're having so much bad workmanship around the place. OK? Then it's drinks, dinner and dancing girls. Got it?'

James Bond said that he understood. He was slightly unsteady on his feet as he walked towards the lobby door and unlocked it. Yes, he understood. Mr Rotkopf was dead. And Bond was the next person on Scaramanga's list. He understood only too well what the situation was.

10

The Dinner Party

B ack in the small office behind the hotel reception desk, James Bond quickly went over the key parts of the meeting with Leiter and Nicholson. They all agreed that they had enough evidence recorded on tape to have Scaramanga locked away in prison for the rest of his life. Leiter planned to follow the men later that night when they got rid of[44] Rotkopf's dead body. He wanted to try and get enough evidence to take Garfinkel and Hendriks to court as well.

Bond returned to his room, poured himself a large whisky and then lay on his bed thinking about the day's events. One thing was certainly clear – he now found himself in a very delicate and dangerous situation.

When Bond joined the others for dinner, he could sense that things had changed. The men now seemed to be avoiding him – they knew the boss did not trust him and wanted him dead. He was certainly not someone they now wanted to be friendly with. The restaurant had been decorated with tropical plants and colourful fruits, and as the men ate their meal a calypso band was playing rather too loudly on the stage. A pretty girl, dressed in a bright red and gold costume and wearing a large, false pineapple on top of her head, was singing a slow song unenthusiastically. Bond was finding the evening extremely boring; the food was unremarkable and the other guests were ignoring him. He got up and went to the head of the table. He told Scaramanga, 'I've got a headache. I'm going to bed.'

'No,' Scaramanga declared quite forcefully, looking coldly at Bond. 'If you think the evening isn't going well, make it go better. That's what you're being paid for. Do something about it.'

It was many years since James Bond had accepted a 'dare'. He felt the eyes of the group watching him, waiting to see what would happen next. Stupidly, he wanted to show these men, who thought him unimportant, what he could do. He did not stop to think that it would have been better for him to keep quiet at that moment. Instead he said decisively, 'All right, Mr Scaramanga. Give me a hundred-dollar note and your gun.'

Scaramanga did not move. He looked up at Bond with surprise and uncertainty. Mr Paradise shouted, 'Come on! Let's see what he can do!'

Scaramanga reached for his wallet and slowly took out a folded hundred-dollar note. Next he carefully reached into his waistband and pulled out his gun. He laid the golden gun and the note on the table in front of him. With his back to the stage, James Bond picked up the gun and checked that it was loaded. At once Bond turned, dropped onto one knee so that his aim would be above the musicians on the stage, and shot the gun. The explosion was deafening and the music stopped immediately. There was a tense silence. What was left of the false pineapple fell to the floor with a thud. A second later, the girl put her hands to her face and slowly fell down onto the floor.

As the men started to comment to each other in low voices, Bond picked up the hundred-dollar note and approached the girl. He lifted her up by her arm and pushed the folded note into her

At once Bond turned, dropped onto one knee so that his aim would be above the musicians on the stage, and shot the gun.

hand. 'That was a fine act we did together. Don't worry. You were in no danger. I aimed for the top half of the pineapple. Now run off and get ready for your next song.' He turned her round and gave her a gentle push. She gave him a horrified glance and ran off into the shadows.

Bond turned to the band. 'All right then, listen to me. This isn't a tea party. Mr Scaramanga's friends want some action and some fun. You can drink as much rum as you want, but you'd better start playing some decent music. I want that pretty girl back, and her friends, and I want them to dance down here near where we're sitting, not up on the stage. Do you understand? Now unless you get moving I'll finish this show now and there'll be no money. OK? Then let's go.'

There was nervous laughter from the band as they exchanged smiles and one of the men ran off after the girl. Bond walked back and laid the pistol down in front of Scaramanga, who gave Bond a long, questioning look and then pushed the gun back into his waistband. After Bond's impressive act, the atmosphere lifted and the evening became a success. It had been a risk, but it had paid off[45], and it wasn't until the early hours of the morning that Bond slipped away back to his room.

With relief, Bond took a shower and climbed into bed. He worried for a while about having shown off[46] with the gun, but it was a stupid mistake that he could not change now. He soon went to sleep and dreamt of three dark figures dragging a shapeless, heavy weight towards dark waters that were full of long, twisting, snapping crocodiles.

11

Unexpected Visitors

A soft tapping sound woke Bond from his restless sleep. It took him a moment to realize that the tapping noise was coming from behind the curtains. He quietly picked up his gun and crept along the wall to the edge of the curtains. He pulled them aside with one quick movement. The golden blonde hair was immediately visible in the moonlight through the half-open window. Mary Goodnight was looking at him through the glass.

Bond breathed a sigh of relief[P]. He put down his gun, carefully opened the window fully and helped Goodnight to climb into the room. There was a bang as the window snapped shut and they both froze. After a moment or two he quietly guided her through the moonlit room and into the bathroom. After closing the door and turning on the taps to cover the sound of their conversation, he said firmly, 'What on earth are you doing here, Mary?'

Her voice was desperate. 'I had to come. I had to find you somehow. I went to that bar and the girl there told me where she thought you'd gone. I left the car in the trees at the bottom of the hotel drive and crept up here. I didn't know where you were, but then I saw the open window and I just somehow knew that you would be the only one to sleep with your window open. So I took the chance.'

'What's happened?' asked Bond.

'There's an urgent message from Headquarters. They said it had to be given to you at all costs[P]. They think you are in Havana, but they said that one of the KGB top men who goes by the name Hendriks is staying at this hotel. You must stay away from him. Apparently one of his jobs is to find you and, er, well, kill you. So I put two and two together[P], and knowing you were in this corner of the island, I thought you might already be on his track, but

49

that you might not know *he* was looking for you, while *you* were looking for him. If that makes sense.'

There was a pause while Bond thought, then he responded. 'Yes, he's here, that's for sure. And so is a gunman called Scaramanga. You might as well know, Mary, that Scaramanga killed Ross in Trinidad.'

She put her hand to her mouth in shock. 'And as for Hendriks,' continued Bond, 'he's here all right, although I don't think he's identified me for certain. But don't worry. I think I can handle the situation. Besides, I've got help.' He told her about Felix Leiter and Nicholson. 'Now, we've got to get you out of here. Just tell Headquarters that you've delivered the message, that I'm here and that the two CIA men are here as well.' With that he gently put a hand on her shoulder, then turned off the taps and opened the bathroom door.

As they stepped back into the room a steady voice came from the darkness at the end of the bed: 'Step forward both of you. Put your hands together behind your head.' Scaramanga walked to the door and turned the lights on. The golden gun remained pointing at Bond as he moved.

Bond looked at him in disbelief. He looked towards the bedroom door – his case was there, as it had been the night before, with the glasses balanced on top. And Scaramanga could not possibly have got through the small window on his own. Then he saw that the wardrobe was open and a light was shining through it from the room next door. It was the simplest of secret doors – just the whole of the back of the cupboard. And it would have been impossible for Bond to discover it while checking his room.

Scaramanga stood looking at both of them. 'I didn't see this dancer on the stage tonight. Where has she come from?' he said accusingly.

'We're engaged to be married,' stated Bond, thinking quickly. 'She's a clerk at the British High Commissioner's Office in Kingston. Her name's Mary Goodnight. She found out where I was staying from that bar where you and I met and came out to tell me that my mother's in hospital in London – she's had a bad fall.' Bond then challenged Scaramanga, adding a note of anger to his voice. 'What's wrong with that? And what do you think you are doing, coming into my room in the middle of the night waving a gun around?' After a pause, he dropped his hands to his sides and turned to the girl. 'Put your hands down, Mary. Mr Scaramanga must have thought there were burglars in here when he heard the window slam shut. Now, you'd better be going. You've got a long drive back to Kingston.'

Mary began to play her part in the story. 'Gosh, yes. I'd better go,' she said as she picked up her small bag from the bed where she had dropped it. 'I really mustn't be late into the office in the morning. I'm organizing a big party for the Prime Minister and it's tomorrow so I've a lot to do. So, Mr – er – Scramble, I'm terribly sorry for waking you up.' And she stepped forward between Bond and Scaramanga and offered him her hand to shake.

But Scaramanga was not going to be taken in so easily. 'Stop there, lady. And you, mister, stay where you are.' Mary Goodnight let her hand fall to her side and looked at him questioningly as though he had just refused a cup of tea. A second passed, yet it felt like an eternity, before Scaramanga conceded. 'OK, I believe you. Put her through the window again.' He waved his gun at the girl. 'OK. Get moving and don't come back.' Bond led Goodnight to the window and hurriedly helped to push her out. Then he moved away from the window and sat down on the bed with considerable relief. He could feel the hard shape of his gun under the pillow against his leg.

Scaramanga had put his gun away and was leaning against the wall. 'The High Commissioner's Office,' he said and paused. 'That also houses the representative of your famous Secret Service, doesn't it? I wonder, Mr Hazard, if your real name isn't James Bond. You were pretty quick with that gun tonight. I seem to have heard somewhere that this man Bond likes his guns. I also have information that he's somewhere in the Caribbean and that he's looking for me. Quite a coincidence, don't you think?'

Bond laughed easily. 'I thought they'd got rid of that Secret Service years ago. I am who I say I am. All you've got to do is call Mr Tony Hugill, the boss up at Frome, and check on my story. And can you explain how this Bond man could possibly have tracked you down to a sleepy bar in Savanna-La-Mar? And what does he want from you anyway?'

Scaramanga watched him silently for a while, weighing up the evidence[P]. Then he spoke in a serious tone. 'You just remember this, mister. If it turns out you're not who you say you are, I'll shoot you dead. Got it?' There was silence while the men looked at each other. Bond said nothing. 'Now you'd better get some sleep,' said Scaramanga. 'I've got a meeting at ten o'clock in the conference room with Hendriks and I don't want to be disturbed. After that we're all going for a ride down to Green Island Harbour on that train I was telling you about. It'll be your job to make sure that the trip is well organized. Talk to the hotel manager first thing in the morning. All right?' Scaramanga did not wait for an answer. He walked into the wardrobe, pushed Bond's suit to one side and disappeared.

12

Bad News

The next morning Bond arrived at the conference room a few minutes before ten o'clock. The evidence of the day before was still there to be seen. The chairs were roughly in their correct positions, but the ashtrays had not been emptied. Bond looked for stains on the carpet, or for signs that the carpet had been washed, but there were none. Rotkopf had probably been killed by a single bullet through the heart. Bond tidied the room and then dutifully started to examine the windows and curtains. At that moment in walked Scaramanga followed by Hendriks. He said roughly, 'OK, Mr Hazard. Lock both doors like yesterday. No one comes in. Right?'

'Yes,' affirmed Bond, and he then went out and locked the door. Again, he fetched a champagne glass and took up his position listening through the door. Immediately, Hendriks began talking, quickly and urgently. 'Mr S, I have bad troubles to report. I spoke with my people in Havana this morning. They have heard direct from Moscow. That man – the man outside this room right now – is the British secret agent, James Bond. They have given me his description and the scar down the right side of his face leaves no doubt. And his shooting last night!' There was a pause and then Hendriks spoke in a calmer, more threatening tone. 'But how can this have happened? What a shocking mistake! If it weren't for the watchfulness of my superiors, who knows what damage this man might have done? I must give my superiors a full report. You must tell me exactly how this man ended up working for you in this way.'

There was silence. Bond imagined Scaramanga sitting back in his chair, looking directly into the eyes of Mr Hendriks. The voice, when it came, was decisive and firm. 'Mr Hendriks, thank you for this information and for your concern. However, tell your people this: I met this man completely by accident, at least I thought so at the time, so there is no point in worrying about how it has happened. It hasn't been easy to set up this conference so quickly and I needed help, someone to make things go smoothly. This guy seemed OK. But I'm not stupid. I knew that when this was all over I'd have to get rid of him, just in case he'd learnt anything he shouldn't have. Now you say he's a member of the Secret Service. What you've told me only changes one thing: he'll die today instead of tomorrow. And here's how it's going to happen …' Scaramanga lowered his voice. Now Bond could only hear a few words of what was being said. The sweat ran down his ear as he pressed it to the bottom of the champagne glass. 'Our train trip ... rats in the sugar cane ... unfortunate accident ... before I do it ... a big laugh ...' There was a pause and then Scaramanga went on in a louder voice, 'So you can relax. There'll be nothing left of the guy by this evening. OK?'

Mr Hendriks' voice was flat and uninterested. He had carried out his orders and definite action was going to follow. 'Yes, what you are saying will be satisfactory. I will watch with amusement. And now I want to talk about other business – the sabotage of the aluminium industry. My superiors want to know what the situation is.'

'Yes,' replied Scaramanga. 'Everything is going to plan with the three aluminium producing companies we agreed on – Reynolds Metal, Kaiser Bauxite and Alumina of Jamaica. The barrels of explosives you gave me are pretty powerful, aren't they? We've already got most of them hidden away in their aluminium mines. They're certainly going to cause a lot of problems for the metal industry and shake the economy here and in the United States.'

'Good. That is all, then,' concluded Hendriks.

'OK. Let's go and see if the others are ready to go out. It's half-past eleven and the train is due to leave in an hour or so,' explained Scaramanga.

Bond moved quickly away from the door and sat on a nearby chair. As Scaramanga unlocked the door and stepped into the room Bond looked up and yawned.

Mr Scaramanga and Mr Hendriks looked down at him with a look of only mild interest. It was as if Bond were a piece of steak and they were wondering whether to have it cooked rare[47] or medium rare.

13

The Train Trip

At twelve o'clock the men all met in the hotel lobby and Scaramanga, now wearing a large, white Stetson cowboy hat and a white suit, announced the plans for the day. 'OK, guys. We're going to have a great time. First we have to drive a couple of kilometres down the road to the station. We'll get aboard this amazing steam train. Then we're going to steam along this old train track through the sugar cane fields for about 30 kilometres until we get to Green Island Harbour. There are plenty of birds, rats and crocodiles in the rivers. We might do a bit of hunting, have some fun with our guns. You've all got your guns with you? Fine, fine. Then we'll have lunch with some champagne at Green Island Harbour, and the music and girls will be there to keep us happy. After lunch we can get aboard the *Thunder Girl* – a big, beautiful motorboat – and we'll go for a cruise and catch ourselves some big fish. Then back here for some drinks. All right? Everyone satisfied? Then let's go.'

As they travelled in the cars to the station, Bond wondered what the plan was for his removal. It would happen during the 'hunting' he presumed and smiled darkly to himself. Strangely, he was feeling happy. He would not have been able to explain the emotion, but it was a feeling of being tightly wound up, like a spring[48] ready to uncoil. After six weeks of following this man, today was the day he was going to win or lose. Scaramanga was just amusing himself and entertaining his friends, whereas Bond was fighting for his life. Surely that would give him the edge[P] when the moment came. Thinking about all of this was beginning to make Bond feel tense. He took a deep breath, told himself to relax and looked out of the window at the passing scenery.

The steam train, called 'The Belle', was an impressive replica[49] black and yellow engine. It stood in the station, shining brightly in the hot midday sun, with a thin line of black smoke curling up from its funnel. Behind the engine was a coal-tender[50] and then there was one carriage, which was open-topped and had several rows of bench seats. The brake van came last and was also painted in black and yellow. It had just one large, golden-armed chair where the guard would normally sit to control the brake wheel of the train.

'All aboard!' cried Scaramanga enthusiastically and then he turned immediately to Bond. 'Now then, you climb up in the front with the driver.'

Bond smiled happily. 'Thanks. I've always wanted to do that since I was a child. What fun!'

Scaramanga ignored the comment and turned to speak to the other men. 'You can all sit in the carriage. Mr Hendriks, you sit in the first row of seats behind the coal-tender, please. The rest of you sit behind him. I'll be at the back in the brake van – it's a good place to hunt from. OK?'

Everybody took their seats. Moments later the engine gave a triumphant TOOT! and the train pulled out of the station. It started to pick up speed as it moved along the track, which disappeared, as straight as an arrow, into the distance.

Bond had studied in detail the map that Mary had given him and he knew exactly the route that the train line took. First there would be 10 kilometres of cane fields, then came Middle River, followed by huge areas of swampland. Then would come Orange River leading into Orange Bay and then more sugar cane and mixed forest and small farms until they came to Green Island Harbour. Now he looked around him and paid careful attention to his immediate surroundings. Next to him stood the driver, who looked dirty and violent. He was shovelling coal into the engine and seemed to have no interest in Bond whatsoever. Bond said, 'My name's Mark Hazard. What's yours?'

The man simply stared at Bond in a way which made it very clear that he did not want to talk. Bond looked back over the low coal-tender to the carriage behind. He gave a cheery wave to the men and shouted, 'Great fun!' They all stared back at him, but not one of them responded to his comment. So, thought Bond, they had been told that he was a spy among them and that he would be killed today! It was an uncomfortable feeling having those ten enemy eyes watching him like ten gun barrels. He rested his hand against his gun, then on the three spare magazines of ammunition he carried in his pocket, and felt reassured.

About 100 metres ahead, a large bird rose up from beside the track and, after a few heavy flaps, caught the wind and moved up and away. There came the BOOM of Scaramanga's gun. A single feather came floating down from the wing of the bird. A second shot was fired. The bird gave a sudden jerk and then began to fall untidily out of the sky before crashing into the sugar cane. There were shouts of joy from the carriage. Bond leant out of the carriage and shouted, 'That'll cost you five pounds. That's the fine for killing a John Crow.'

A shot whistled past Bond's head. Scaramanga laughed. 'Sorry. I thought I saw a rat!' Then another shot rang out as Bond jumped down out of sight and the other men began to laugh. 'Watch what you're saying, man,' Scaramanga shouted to Bond, 'or I really will shut you up.'

Beside Bond the driver swore and then sounded the train's whistle. Bond looked down the line. Far ahead, there was something lying across the rails of the track. With the train still whistling, the driver pulled back hard on the accelerator lever. The train began to slow down, but then Scaramanga fired two shots into the air and yelled, 'Keep going fast, you idiot!'

The driver quickly pushed up the lever and, alarmingly, the train began to regain its speed. He glanced at Bond and commented flatly, 'There's a girl on the line. I guess it must be some friend of the boss.'

Bond leant out and looked more carefully. Yes! It was a woman. A woman with golden blonde hair!

Bond heard Scaramanga's voice shouting from the brake van, 'Hey, guys. It's a surprise for you all. Something from the good old Western films. There's a girl tied across the line. And you know what? It's the girlfriend of a certain man we've been hearing of called James Bond. Would you believe it? And her name's Goodnight, Mary Goodnight. If only that man Bond were on the train now, I imagine we'd be hearing him cry out to save her.'

14

The Swamplands

James Bond threw himself towards the accelerator lever and pushed it down with all his strength. The engine lost some of its power, but there were only 100 metres between the train and the girl. The only thing that could save the girl was if Scaramanga used the brakes in the last van. She was going to die! Bond, knowing that Scaramanga would expect him to come out from the right side of the engine, jumped to the left. Hendriks had his gun out, but before he could turn, Bond shot a bullet straight between the man's cold eyes. The head was knocked back and his body fell to one side. Scaramanga's golden gun fired two shots. A bullet crashed into the cabin of the engine. The second struck the driver, who fell to the ground, screaming.

There were only 50 metres of track left! The golden hair was blowing over the face and Bond could clearly see the rope tied around the ankles and wrists. Bond shut his mind to the dreadful crash that would come any moment now. He leant out of the left side of the cabin again and fired three more shots. He thought two of them had found their targets, but then he felt a great blow to his shoulder, which knocked him to the floor of the cabin, his head hanging out of the train. And it was from there, only a couple of metres away, that he saw the front wheels of the engine crash through the body on the line. He saw the blonde head cut from the body, saw the blue glass eyes give him a last empty stare, saw the pieces of the shop window dummy[51] break into bits with a sharp cracking of plastic and fall into the grass beside the track.

James Bond, relieved that it had not been Mary on the track, but feeling sick and shocked, struggled to get to his feet. He reached for the accelerator lever and pushed it upwards as far as it would go. He thought that a gun battle against five men on a stationary train would be difficult for him, but he would have a better chance of survival on a fast, moving train. He hardly felt the pain in his shoulder. He looked out of the right-hand side of the engine. Four guns boomed. Bond threw himself back under cover, but he had just had time to see a glorious sight. In the brake van, Scaramanga had slid from the large chair and was down on his knees looking as though he was in pain. Bond's bullet had hit him. It was very good news, but there were still four armed men remaining.

Then a voice from the back of the train – Felix Leiter's voice – called out, 'OK, you four guys. Throw your guns over the side. Now! Quick!' There came the boom of a shot. 'I said quick! There – Mr Gengerella is dead. Do the rest of you want to go the same way? OK, then. That's better. And now put your hands behind your heads. Right. OK, James, the battle's over. Are you OK? Show yourself.'

Bond rose carefully. He could hardly believe it! Leiter must have been riding secretly on the buffers[52] behind the brake van. He would not have been able to show himself earlier for fear of Bond's gunfire. Yes! It was definitely Leiter! He was standing beside the now fallen body of Scaramanga and pointing his pistol at the three surviving men in the carriage. Bond's shoulder had really begun to hurt now. He shouted, with the anger of huge

*It was definitely Leiter! He was standing beside
the now fallen body of Scaramanga.*

relief, 'Thanks a lot, Leiter. Why on earth didn't you show up before? I could have been hurt.'

Leiter laughed. 'That'll be the day!ᴾ Now listen. Get ready to jump. I'm going to stay with these guys for a while and hand them over to the police in Green Island Harbour.' At this point he shook his head silently to show Bond that these words were actually a lie. 'It's swampland, so you'll have a soft landing. It stinks a bit, but don't worry, we'll give you some aftershave when you get home. All right?'

Bond looked ahead down the line. In the distance he could see the metal structure of the Orange River bridge. He looked back into the carriage. He could see the dead body of Hendriks, rolling from side to side on the bench. In the seat behind Hendriks, Gengerella also lay dead. Next to him and behind him, the other three gangsters looked terrified. They had not expected all this. They were in serious trouble and they knew it.

Bond gave these cold men, who had been prepared to murder him, one last look before he got down onto the steps of the cabin, ready to jump. He chose his moment and threw himself clear of the train and into the soft, wet mass of the stinking mangrove swamp.

As he fell a bird gave a loud screech and flew up and away. The stink was unbearable. He raised his head in time to see Leiter, some 200 metres away, throw himself off the brake van. He seemed to land clumsily and did not get up. And now, within only a few metres of the long metal bridge, another man jumped from the train. It was a tall figure wearing a white jacket. There was no doubt about it! It was Scaramanga! Why on earth had Leiter left the train without putting a finishing bullet through the man's head? The fight was not over yet.

Bond watched as the track began to take the steam train across the bridge. He wondered what would happen to those three men. Perhaps the train would run out of steam and they would run away to the hills. Or could they get the train under control and go on to Green Island Harbour and try and take the motorboat over to Cuba? Immediately the answer came. Halfway across the bridge, the engine suddenly rose up into the air. At the same time there came a crash of thunder and a huge sheet of flames, before the bridge started to collapse. Bond watched as the bridge folded in on itself and the train crashed down into the river.

A terrible silence fell. A bird then began to sing and two butterflies lazily flew past Bond where he lay. His shoulder was causing him a great deal of pain, but he got slowly to his feet, pulled himself out of the wet mud and began walking up the track towards the bridge.

Leiter lay in the stinking swamp. His left leg was at a hideous angle. Bond knew that it was badly broken. He knelt down by the man and said softly, 'I can't do much for you now. I'll give you a bullet to bite on for the pain and get you into some shade. There'll be people coming soon. I've got to follow Scaramanga. He's somewhere up there by the bridge. What made you think he was dead?'

Leiter groaned, more with anger with himself than from the pain. 'There was blood all over the place. And I thought that if he wasn't dead already, the bridge would put an end to him.' He gave Bond a weak smile. 'Did you like what I'd planned for the bridge? Did it get rid of the train OK?'

Bond smiled in return. 'It was a fabulous fireworks display. The crocodiles will be sitting down to their dinner right now. But that shop dummy! That gave me a real shock. Did you put it on the track?'

'Ah, yes. Sorry about that, James. I had no idea your girlfriend was blonde, or that you'd believe it was her. Mr S told me to tie the thing to the track and as I'm supposed to be the assistant manager, I couldn't refuse. But it gave me the excuse I needed to get the explosives under the bridge this morning.'

'Stupid of me, I suppose,' admitted Bond. 'I thought he'd caught her last night. Anyway, come on. Here, bite on this bullet.

This is going to hurt, but I must get you under cover and out of the sun.' Bond put his hands under Leiter's armpits and dragged him, as carefully as he could, to a dry patch under a big mangrove bush. Leiter gave a groan as he fainted from the pain. Bond looked thoughtfully down at him. Fainting was probably the best thing that could happen to him right now. He took Leiter's gun out of his waistband and put it beside his left, and only, hand. Bond was still in a lot of danger. If he ended up dead, then Scaramanga would certainly make Felix his second target.

Bond started to creep along the line of mangrove bushes towards the bridge. It was early afternoon now and the sun was high. He was hungry and very thirsty and his shoulder wound was hurting as he moved. He struggled to remain focused on what he had to do. About 100 metres lay between him and the bridge. He covered another 20 by walking near the track then moved sideways into the mangroves. He found that if he kept close to the roots of the bushes he could move fairly easily and silently. His ears were alert, like an animal, ready to hear the smallest sound. Bond guessed that he had gone about 200 metres into the swamp when he heard a single, controlled cough.

15

The End of the Road[P]

The cough sounded as though it was about 20 metres away towards the river. Bond dropped to one knee, listening intently, looking all around. He waited for five minutes without moving. When the cough was not repeated, he crept forward on his hands and knees, his gun gripped between his teeth.

In a small clearing[53] of dried, cracked mud, he saw the man. Bond stopped in his tracks, trying to calm his breathing.

Scaramanga was lying stretched out, his back resting against a large mangrove root. His hat had gone and the whole of the right side of his white suit was dark with blood, yet the man's eyes were still very much alive. They swept the clearing every few seconds, looking for any signs of movement in the swamp. His hands rested on the roots beside him, Bond noticed. And there was no sign of a gun.

After a while, Scaramanga, very carefully, coughed again and spat into his hand. He examined the bright pink results and threw them down onto the ground. The cough did not seem to hurt him or cause him much effort. Bond guessed that his bullet had hit Scaramanga in the right side of his chest and had just missed a lung. There was bleeding, but the blood-soaked jacket was not telling the whole truth. In Bond's opinion, Mr Scaramanga was still very much alive and dangerous.

Bond was grateful that he was wearing a dark-coloured suit. He was well camouflaged and Scaramanga had not seen him. He got quietly up from his knees, put the gun in his right hand and, keeping his gaze firmly on Scaramanga, he strolled slowly out into the clearing. The other man barely looked up, but said, 'You've taken your time getting here.' He nodded his head towards the gun and added, 'You're not frightened of a dying man, are you? You Brits are pretty cowardly.'

Bond ignored the comment and walked a little closer. 'Have you got any more weapons on you? Open your jacket. Slowly! No quick movements. Show me your belt. Now your armpits … and your trouser legs.' As Scaramanga moved his trouser leg Bond caught sight of a shining blade. 'Right. Just throw that knife gently into the trees. Gently – very gently.'

Scaramanga took the knife and, with a flick of his wrist, threw the knife upwards. The silver blade went spinning like a wheel through the sunshine. Bond had to step aside, and the knife landed, blade downwards, in the mud, exactly where Bond had been standing. Scaramanga gave a cold laugh, then the laugh turned into a cough and his face twisted with the terrible pain of it. Or was he faking it? Then he relaxed again.

'Now, then,' began Bond. 'Let's talk. You've killed too many of my friends. I have the licence to kill you and that's what I am going to do. But I'll make it quick. Not like Margesson. Do you remember him? You were stupid enough to boast about killing him to your friends in Cuba and we heard about it.' Bond paused and then asked, 'As a matter of interest, how many men have you killed in your life?'

'With you, it'll be exactly fifty,' replied Scaramanga. He looked up at Bond and said, 'You won't get any secrets out of me, if that's what you're trying to do. I've been shot at by all kinds of experts and I'm still alive. I've never heard of a Brit who's got the guts to shoot a wounded, defenceless man. I bet we'll just sit here chatting until the rescue team get here. Then I'll be glad to go to court. What will they get me for, anyway?'

'Well, just for a start, there's that nice Mr Rotkopf with one of your famous gold and silver bullets in him in the river at the back of your hotel.'

'That matches the nice Mr Hendriks with one of *your* bullets somewhere in him. Maybe we'll spend a bit of time in prison together. That'd be nice, wouldn't it? And anyway, who says I killed Rotkopf?' Scaramanga asked.

'It seems you've made quite a few mistakes recently, Mr Scaramanga. You hired all the wrong security men. Both of your managers were from the CIA. They bugged all of your phones and your conference room. The recording of the gunshot and the conversation about getting rid of Rotkopf's body will be on its way to the CIA headquarters by now. The recordings also include you admitting to the murder of one of our best agents, Ross, of course. See what I mean? There's no way out.'

'OK, mister secret agent, mistakes seem to have been made. So, then. Take one million dollars, let me go and let's call it a deal,' offered Scaramanga.

'I don't think so,' refused Bond as he prepared himself to take the other man's life. 'This is the end of the road for you.' He forced himself to think of the people that this man had killed, of the people he would go on to kill in the future if Bond weakened. This man was the most dangerous, cruel and efficient one-man killer in the world. Bond had been instructed to kill him. He must kill him – lying down wounded, or in any other position. Although nervous, Bond tried to appear casual. 'Any messages for anyone, Scaramanga? Anyone you want looking after? I'll take care of it if it's personal. I'll keep that information to myself.'

Scaramanga laughed his cold laugh, but carefully. 'What an English gentleman you are!' A few long moments passed without either man speaking. Scaramanga lay breathing steadily against the mangrove root. Bond stood with sweat dripping from his face and his gun pointing at the man.

Then Scaramanga held up a hand. For the first time his face showed emotion and he spoke softly, 'Just let me say one last prayer, OK? It won't take long and then you can fire your bullets.'

James Bond lowered his gun. He decided that he would give the man a few minutes, but no longer. 'Go ahead,' he uttered in a tired voice, 'one minute only.'

Scaramanga's hand came up and covered his face. There came murmurings in Latin, which seemed to go on for a long time. Bond stood there in the sunshine, his gun lowered, watching Scaramanga, but at the same time not really watching him. The pain in his shoulder, the heat, his thirst and the thought of what he was about to do all began to distract him.

The fingers of Scaramanga's right hand crawled ever so slowly sideways across his face, centimetre by centimetre. They got to his ear and stopped. The murmuring of the prayer carried on exactly as before.

And then the hand leapt behind the head and a tiny golden handgun fired loudly. Bond spun round as if he had taken a punch to the right side of his face and then he crashed to the ground.

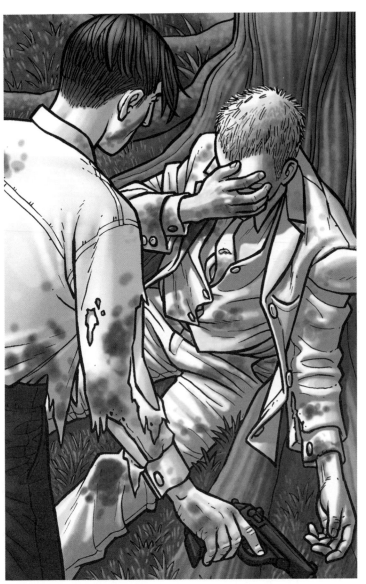

Scaramanga's hand came up and covered his face.

At once Scaramanga was on his feet and was moving forward quickly like a cat. He grabbed the knife he had thrown away earlier and held it in front of him in a threatening way.

Bond was twisting on the ground like a dying animal and the gun in his hand cracked loudly again and again – five times. Then the gun fell sideways onto the black earth as his gun-hand went to the right side of his body and stayed there, grabbing at the terrible pain there.

The big man stood for a moment and looked up at the deep blue sky. His fingers opened suddenly and let go of the knife. His heart, shot through by a bullet, stopped beating and he crashed backwards. Now he lay unmoving, his arms out wide to the sides, as if someone had thrown him away.

16

The Case Ends

A week later, James Bond slowly opened his eyes. He was confused and anxious and did not know where he was. He opened his mouth to scream but only a low groan came out. The nurse at the end of the bed stood up at once and went to his side and put a cool hand on his forehead. Bond looked up at her with unfocused eyes and muttered, 'You're pretty,' before closing his eyes again.

Half an hour later a young doctor stood outside the door to Bond's hospital room in Kingston, explaining to the head nurse what he had found. 'He's going to be all right. His temperature is down now. His pulse[54] is a little fast, though that may have been a result of his waking up. I'll come back later to check his wounds. He's likely to wake up again. If he does and he asks for something to drink, give him fruit juice. He should be on soft foods soon. It's a miracle really. The bullet just hit muscle and didn't even touch a kidney. But that bullet was dipped in enough poison to kill a horse. Thank goodness that doctor in Savanna-La-Mar recognized the symptoms of snake venom and gave him those powerful anti-snakebite injections. He saved the man's life. Now then, there should be no visitors, of course. I'll tell the police and the High Commissioner's Office that he's recovering. I don't know who this Mr Bond is, but apparently London keep calling us about him. He's something to do with the Ministry of Defence.' He paused. 'By the way, how's his friend getting on in room 12 – Mr Leiter, isn't it? The one the American Ambassador and Washington have been calling about? He keeps on asking to see this Mr Bond.'

'He's broken his leg in several places,' replied the nurse. 'He's doing fine and should be walking with a stick in ten days. He's already seen the police. I suppose it's all connected with that story in the papers about those American tourists being killed when the bridge collapsed near Green Island Harbour. The Police Commissioner is handling the case himself.'

———

Ten days later, the small hospital room was crowded with people. Bond, who was being supported by a pile of pillows, was amused by the number of official people who had been brought to his bedside. On his left was the Commissioner of Police, who was wearing full uniform complete with a row of very impressive-looking medals. On his right was a Judge of the Supreme Court, who was also very formally dressed and was accompanied by a clerk. Among the rest, a huge man, to whom Felix Leiter, on crutches[55], was quite respectful, had been introduced to Bond as Colonel Bannister from Washington. Mary Goodnight was also there and had been asked to take notes of the meeting. She had also been asked by the nurse to watch for any signs of tiredness or discomfort in James Bond and had been given the authority to end the meeting if she felt it necessary. But James Bond did not feel tired. He was delighted to see all these people and to know at last that he was very much alive. The only thing that concerned him was that he and Leiter had not been able to see each other and agree their stories before this meeting. They had carried out this dangerous mission without the knowledge of the Jamaican authorities. A couple of years ago, when Jamaica had still been under British rule, that would have been fine. But now, Bond knew, things were different. They had been wrong not to keep the Police Commissioner informed.

The Police Commissioner straightened himself and began to speak in a formal tone. 'Commander Bond, our meeting here today is being held on the Prime Minister's instructions and with your doctor's approval. There are many rumours going around the island and we are keen to understand exactly what happened so that justice can be carried out. So, this meeting takes the form of a judicial inquiry[56]. I will outline the facts of the case, Mary Goodnight will take notes and then a formal document will be prepared. We very much hope that, if the conclusions of the meeting are satisfactory, the case will be closed. Do you understand?'

'Yes,' said Bond, who did not understand.

'Now,' the Commissioner said in a serious tone. 'The facts we know are as follows. There recently took place, at the Thunderbird Hotel, a meeting of what can only be described as foreign gangsters of the worst kind, including representatives of the Soviet Secret Service, the Mafia and the Cuban Secret Police. They met to discuss the sabotage of the Jamaican sugar cane and aluminium industries, among other related things. Am I correct, Commander?'

'Yes,' agreed Bond quickly. At least this part was true.

'Now.' The Commissioner spoke in an even more serious tone. 'Knowledge of this meeting came to the attention of the Criminal Investigation Department of the Jamaican Police. Secret

70

conversations then took place between the Jamaican authorities, the Ministry of Defence in Britain and the Central Intelligence Agency in the United States. As a result of these conversations, you, Mr Nicholson and Mr Leiter were sent to help us to uncover these secret plans against Jamaica.' As the man spoke, Bond noticed that Leiter was nodding his head enthusiastically and looking directly into Bond's eyes. Bond smiled. Leiter was clearly trying to tell him that they should both agree with these comments, which were not true. They both knew that there had never been any contact with the Jamaican authorities.

'Working very closely with the Jamaican authorities,' the Commissioner went on, 'Mr Bond, Mr Nicholson and Mr Leiter carried out their duties with professionalism. They uncovered the true intentions of the gangsters, but unfortunately during their mission at least one of their identities was discovered and a battle then took place. During the battle the following enemy agents (the finished report will include a list here) were killed thanks to the skilful gunfire of Commander Bond and Mr Leiter; and the following enemy agents (there will be another list here) were killed by Mr Leiter's use of explosives on Orange River Bridge. Unfortunately, Commander Bond and Mr Leiter received severe wounds, from which they are now recovering in the Kingston Memorial Hospital. Finally, it must be noted that Constable Percival Sampson of the Negril Constabulary was the first to discover the wounded Felix Leiter, who then directed Constable Sampson to the scene of the final fight.

'On the instructions of the Prime Minister, Sir Alexander Bustamante, a judicial inquiry was held today at the bedside of Commander Bond, with Felix Leiter present, to confirm the above facts. These facts, in the presence of Justice Morris Cargill of the Supreme Court, are here and now confirmed.'

The Commissioner was obviously pleased with how the formalities had gone. He smiled broadly at Bond. 'There's just one more thing,' he added as he handed Bond a sealed[57] packet,

71

another similar one to Felix and a third to Colonel Bannister. 'I present now to Commander James Bond of Great Britain, Mr Felix Leiter of the United States and, in his absence, Mr Nicholas Nicholson of the United States, the award of the Jamaican Police Medal for gallant and meritorious services[58] to the independent State of Jamaica.'

Those watching began to clap in recognition of the men's bravery, and James Bond and Felix Leiter muttered a few words of thanks. Justice Cargill rose to his feet and, in a serious tone, asked Bond and Leiter in turn, 'Is this a true and correct account of what happened?'

'Yes, indeed it is,' said Bond.

'Yes, it is, Your Honour,' agreed Leiter enthusiastically.

'In that case,' Justice Cargill announced formally, 'I declare this inquiry closed.' He then turned to Mary Goodnight. 'Please could you ask everyone here to sign this document and then have it delivered to my office? Thank you so much.'

'Certainly, Your Honour,' replied Mary Goodnight and then she glanced at Bond. 'But now, if you don't mind, I think Mr Bond needs to rest.'

Slowly everyone stood up and left the room. Everyone that is, apart from Leiter, who waited until he was alone with Bond and then moved closer to his bedside. 'Well, James, that was the easiest inquiry I've ever attended!' exclaimed Leiter. 'I lied my head off, but we've come out of it looking good and we've even been given an award!'

Bond's wounds were beginning to hurt and he felt exhausted. He smiled, trying to hide the pain. Leiter was going to leave Jamaica that afternoon, but Bond did not want to say goodbye. Bond treasured his good friends, and Felix and he had shared a lot of important things over the years. Bond said, 'Scaramanga was quite a guy. If only we could have caught him alive.'

'What ... and make a hero out of him? I don't think so. In my book, an enemy's an enemy. You did the right thing killing that man. You did a good job, so don't you worry about it.' Leiter limped towards the door and opened it. He raised his hand briefly. The two men had never shaken hands in their lives. His final words were, 'And keep away from me for a few weeks. Every time I see you a piece of me gets broken off. I don't like the idea of myself as The Vanishing Man.' He smiled and left the room.

17

Mary Goodnight

Just over a week later, James Bond was sitting up in a chair reading a book and wondering when he was going to be able to leave the hospital. He was feeling much better, and although the nurses were fabulous, especially the pretty one who had been with him when he had woken up, he had had enough of the place. He glanced at his watch. Four o'clock. It was visiting time and Mary Goodnight would be there any minute. Although he knew it was not fair, he was looking forward to complaining at length to her about his situation.

Mary Goodnight came through the door. Despite the Jamaican heat, she was looking as fresh as a rose. Under her arm she was carrying a medium-sized, official-looking envelope with an elaborate wax seal on it.

Bond gave one-word answers to her questions about his health and then demanded, 'What's in that envelope?'

'It's a top secret message for you from M,' she said excitedly.

'Open it for me,' ordered Bond.

Mary Goodnight looked shocked. 'But I'm not allowed to!' Bond gave her a look which told her that today was not a day to argue with him. She carefully opened the envelope, pulled out the thick sheet of paper and began to read.

TOP SECRET
To: 007
From: M

I have received your report and the report from our partners. You have done well and carried out an exceptionally difficult and dangerous mission to my total satisfaction. I trust you are in good health. Please inform me when you will be reporting for your next mission.

'In good health?' interrupted Bond incredulously.

Mary Goodnight looked up and smiled delightedly. 'I've never known him to be so complimentary. Have you, James? It's wonderful!' She looked hopefully at James, yet his face remained expressionless.

She looked down and began to read the message again. 'Oh, James!' She exploded with excitement.

'Don't tell me,' commented Bond in a voice heavy with sarcasm. 'He's going to give me free lunch vouchers every second Friday. And a new suit to replace the one that I've carelessly allowed to get damaged.' But secretly what Mary had read out had delighted him and he very much wanted to know what was in the rest of the message.

'James, please stop interrupting, and don't look so miserable,' said Mary Goodnight.

Bond allowed a smile to creep onto his face. He liked the fact that she could get so excited on his behalf. As he watched her concentrating on the letter, Bond thought that she was someone he would always want to have near him. But as what? As his secretary? As his girlfriend? Mary Goodnight looked up at him and the question, as it had done for weeks, remained without an answer. 'All right, Mary. Go on,' Bond finally said.

Mary Goodnight's face became serious. 'Now just listen to this,' she told him and then began to read the remaining part of the message.

In view of the outstanding quality of the services mentioned above, the Prime Minister plans to recommend to Her Majesty Queen Elizabeth that she immediatley grant you a knighthood[59]. This would be in addition to the KCMG[60] that you already hold. As is usual, I am writing now to accept this high honour before Her Majesty puts her seal upon it. You should first send telegraphed confirmation of acceptance and then follow this with a formal written letter. I am of course in full agreement with this award and send you my personal congratulations.

Of course James Bond was pleased. Above all he was pleased that M had been so complimentary about what he had done. The rest of the message was not important to him. He was not interested in medals or being able to write special letters after his name. He had never been a public figure and he did not want to become one now. There was one thing he treasured above everything else, and that was his privacy.

So now James Bond said to Mary Goodnight, avoiding her eyes, 'Write down what I am about to say and send it in a telegram tonight. All right?'

'Yes, of course,' replied Goodnight with enthusiasm.

Bond began, 'Top secret. For M's eyes only. Your message has been received and greatly appreciated. Am informed by hospital that I shall be returning to London able to work in one month. Regarding the high honour, please ask Her Majesty to allow me to refuse the honour that Her Majesty is kind enough to consider awarding her obedient servant. My main reason for refusing this honour is that I do not want to pay more at hotels and restaurants.'

Mary Goodnight interrupted Bond, horrified by what he was saying. 'James! It is your decision what you write in the rest of the letter, but you really can't say that last part.'

Bond nodded. 'If you say so. Let's change the whole of that last sentence to this: I am a Scottish peasant[61] and will always feel comfortable being a Scottish peasant and I know, sir, that you will understand my preference. A formal letter will follow.'

Mary Goodnight closed her notepad with a snap. She looked at Bond angrily. 'Well really, James! Why don't we talk about this tomorrow. You are clearly in a bad mood and might feel differently in the morning.'

'It's just not my sort of thing,' Bond told her apologetically. 'I just refuse to call myself "Sir James Bond". It's ridiculous. And I know M will understand. He thinks much the same way about these things as I do. Anyway, I'm not going to change my mind, so you can telegraph that straight away and I'll write the letter this evening. Anything else?'

'Well, there is one thing, James,' she said more softly. 'The head nurse said you can leave hospital at the end of the week, but that you really need to rest somewhere quiet for at least three weeks. Have you got any plans for where you might go? You need to be near the hospital.'

'I've no idea. What do you suggest?' enquired Bond.

'Well, er, I've got a little villa up by Mona dam.' She spoke more quickly now, her cheeks reddening a little with embarrassment. 'It's got quite a nice spare room looking out over Kingston harbour. It's cool up there. You could relax and I would cook for you.'

James Bond looked at Mary for a moment and said, and meant it, 'Mary Goodnight, you're an angel.'

At the same time, he knew, deep down, that love from Mary Goodnight, or from any other woman, was not enough for him. The kind of life he had led and the things he had seen had made Bond quite different from most other men. He knew he would always need something more, although he would perhaps never know what exactly that 'something' was.

Points For Understanding

1

1 James Bond's previous mission is described in this chapter. Are these facts true or false? Explain your answers.
   (a) Bond had been sent to get intelligence from the Soviet Union about the Japanese.
   (b) The mission was not a success.
   (c) The British Secret Service knew that Bond had been captured by the Russians.
   (d) Colonel Boris worked at the British Secret Service Headquarters.
2 This chapter is called 'Can I help you?' Who asked this question and what was the answer?
3 Captain Walker pressed two buttons on his phone. What did each button do?
4 Two physical checks were carried out on Bond, and the results given, in this chapter. What were the checks and what did each one reveal?

2

1 'I don't like the feel of this at all.' Why was the Chief of Staff worried?
2 M referred to a 'new safety device'. What was this safety device and what important role did it play in this chapter?
3 Why do you think the KGB got 'very excited' when they checked Bond's fingerprints?
4 Why was it significant that Bond used the word 'we' rather than 'I' when he was explaining why he had come back to London? What other signs were there during this chapter that Bond was not feeling himself?

5   What decision did M take at the end of this chapter, and
    why?

3

1   Francisco Scaramanga's life story is given in this chapter.
    Answer these questions.
    (a) How many British secret agents had he killed?
    (b) By what name was he generally known, and why?
    (c) In which country was he most recently known to have
    lived?
2   The report recommended that Scaramanga should be
    'removed' as soon as possible. What do you think is meant
    by the word 'removed' and why did the writer of the report
    choose to use that word?
3   'For about five minutes he sat and gazed across the room.'
    What do you think M was thinking during this time?

4

1   'Bond could not believe his eyes.' What did Bond find at the
    airport and why was it important?
2   What might the initials SLM have stood for?
3   Bond asked Mary Goodnight for a car and a map. What do
    you think Bond was planning to do with these two things?
4   Mary Goodnight mentioned three people and three places.
    Match each person to a place and then explain who the
    person is and what their connection is to that place:
    (a) Fidel Castro   (1) Frome, Jamaica
    (b) Tony Hugill   (2) Trinidad
    (c) Commander Ross   (3) Russia

5

1 'He likes to make people angry and then …' How do you think Tiffy might have completed her sentence? Why do you think she chose not to complete it?
2 Why was Bond so sure that it was Francisco Scaramanga when the man walked into the room?
3 Describe Bond's first meeting with Scaramanga.

6

1 Bond used the word 'circus' again on purpose. Why?
2 A metal chair is mentioned in this chapter. Who used it and why was it significant?
3 Most of what Bond told Scaramanga in this chapter was not true. Which one of the following things did Bond tell the truth about?
   (a) his name
   (b) who he worked for
   (c) that he carried a gun
   (d) that he did not know who Scaramanga was
4 'So you're trapped – you haven't got the money to finish it and presumably it's not easy to sell.' What was Bond referring to, and why was it a problem for Scaramanga?
5 'Bond could not stop himself from laughing.' Why? What was funny about the situation Bond now found himself in?

7

1 What was the first law a secret agent should follow?
2 Bond searched his hotel room. What did he find and what did he do with what he found?
3 Bond asked himself some questions. Which two things was he unsure about?

4 Several times were mentioned in this chapter. Explain why each of these times was significant:
   (a) half-past seven (b) 10 am (c) midday (d) 4 pm
5 Scaramanga told Bond about six men. Give the names of these men and explain why they were coming to visit Scaramanga.

8

1 'He felt a wave of excitement pass through him.' Explain why Bond was feeling positive at this time.
2 In this chapter Bond guessed that Mr Hendriks must be part of either the Mafia or the KGB. What things led him to that conclusion?
3 Bond was surprised to see a man he had not had contact with for a long time. Who was this man and how did Bond know him originally?
4 At the end of this chapter Bond is described as being 'hugely relieved'. What was the reason for this?

9

1 Which organizations did these people work for?
   (a) Mr Hendriks (b) Nick Nicholson (c) Mr Gengerella
2 Bond picked up a champagne glass in this chapter. What did he use it for?
3 Bond overheard information about Commander Ross during the conference. What had happened to Ross, according to Scaramanga?
4 Someone was killed in this chapter. Who died? How were they killed, and why?
5 'He was slightly unsteady on his feet as he walked towards the lobby door and unlocked it.' What do you think had shocked Bond?

10

1 'They all agreed that they had enough evidence recorded on tape to have Scaramanga locked away in prison for the rest of his life.' Who agreed this and what evidence were they referring to?
2 Explain why Bond said, 'I've got a headache. I'm going to bed.'
3 Explain what Bond did with the hundred-dollar note and Scaramanga's gun.
4 How did the following people react to what Bond did and said? (a) the girl on stage (b) the band members (c) Scaramanga
5 Bond returned to his room and 'soon went to sleep and dreamt of three dark figures …' Who do you think these three dark figures represented?

11

1 This chapter is called 'Unexpected Visitors'. Who were the unexpected visitors and how did they enter the room?
2 Why did Bond go into the bathroom and turn the taps on?
3 What important message had Mary Goodnight come to deliver? Who was the message from?
4 What message did Bond ask Mary Goodnight to return with?
5 What warning did Scaramanga give Bond?

12

1 What bad news did Scaramanga receive in this chapter?
2 What bad news did Bond receive in this chapter?
3 Explain the 'other business' which Scaramanga was carrying out on behalf of Mr Hendriks and his superiors.

13

1 Bond travelled on a train in this chapter. What are the following?
  (a) a coal-tender (b) a brake van (c) an accelerator lever
2 Why was the fact that Scaramanga chose to sit in the brake van important?
3 There are several numbers quoted in this chapter. Explain what each of the following refers to:
  (a) a couple of kilometres (b) 30 kilometres
  (c) 10 kilometres (d) 100 metres (e) five pounds
4 How many gunshots were fired in this chapter? How many of these shots hit their target?

14

1 Put these events in the correct order:
  (a) Bond was injured.
  (b) Bond realized that Mary Goodnight was not dead.
  (c) The train driver was shot.
  (d) Scaramanga was shot.
  (e) Mr Hendriks was shot.
  (f) Bond realized that Leiter was on the train.
2 Mary Goodnight was tied across the train track. True or false?
3 Leiter laughed and then used an English expression, 'That'll be the day!' What did Leiter mean when he said this?
4 Which three men jumped off the train? Of these three men, who landed nearest the bridge and who landed furthest away from it?
5 How many men were left on the train when it crashed? How many of these men were already dead before the train crashed?

15

1 What weapons did Scaramanga have in this chapter and what did he do with them?
2 It was clear to Bond that Scaramanga was a dying man. True or false?
3 Bond mentioned a man called Margesson. Who do you think this man was?
4 What deal did Scaramanga try to make with Bond?

16

1 Bond was lucky to be alive. Who had acted quickly to save his life and what had that person done?
2 Who had asked for the official meeting and what was the purpose of that meeting?
3 Bond and Leiter were worried about something in this chapter. What were they worried about, and why? How did this situation resolve itself?
4 'Every time I see you a piece of me gets broken off.' What was Leiter referring to when he said this?

17

1 Describe how you think both Bond and Mary Goodnight were feeling when she arrived at his hospital room.
2 Bond had mixed feelings about M's message. Explain what those feelings were and what had caused them.
3 'Mary Goodnight interrupted Bond, horrified by what he was saying.' What had Bond said and why had it shocked Mary Goodnight so much?

Glossary

1 **villain** (page 4)
   the main bad character in a story, play, film etc.
2 **gambling** (page 5)
   if you *gamble*, you risk money in the hope of winning more if
   you are lucky. This activity is called *gambling*.
3 **democracy** (page 6)
   a system of government in which people vote in elections to
   choose the people who will govern them
4 **atomic bomb** (page 6)
   a bomb that causes a very large nuclear explosion from the
   energy it produces by breaking atoms apart
5 **conference** (page 7)
   a large meeting, often lasting a few days, where people who
   are interested in a particular subject or who are involved
   in the same thing because of their work come together to
   discuss ideas
6 **penultimate** (page 7)
   the thing that is the one before the last in a series
7 **missile** (page 7)
   a weapon that travels under its own power for long distances
   and explodes when it hits its target
8 **brainwash** – *to brainwash someone* (page 9)
   to force someone to accept a particular set of beliefs by
   repeating the same idea many times so that the person
   cannot think in an independent way
9 **torture** (page 9)
   extreme physical pain caused by someone or something,
   especially as a punishment or as a way to make someone say
   or do something
10 **trace the call** – *to trace a call* (page 10)
   to use electronic equipment to find out where a telephone
   call was made

11 **laboratory** (page 11)

a building or large room where people do scientific and medical experiments or research

12 **device** (page 13)

a machine or piece of equipment that does a particular thing

13 **intercom** (page 13)

a system or a piece of electrical equipment that allows people in different parts of a building, aircraft or ship to speak to each other

14 **bulletproof** (page 15)

made from a material that stops bullets from passing through

15 **poison** (page 16)

a substance that can kill you or make you ill if you eat, drink or breathe it

16 **sedative** (page 18)

a drug that makes someone calmer or makes them sleep

17 **assassin** (page 18)

someone who kills a famous or important person, especially for political reasons, or someone who is paid to kill a particular person

18 **ruthless** (page 19)

willing to make other people suffer so that you can achieve your aims

19 **rival** (page 19)

a person or group that competes against someone or something else

20 **sugar cane crop** (page 23)

a *crop* is a plant grown for food, usually on a farm. *Sugar cane* is a tall tropical plant with a thick stem that is used for producing sugar.

21 **shilling** (page 24)

a small unit of money that used to be used in the UK and some other countries under British rule. *Sixpence* was worth half a *shilling*.

22 **cop** (page 27)

an informal word for a police officer

23 **labour relations** (page 28)

the actions that are taken and the relationships that exist
between employers and the people who work for them

24 **insurance investigation** (page 28)

insurance is an arrangement in which you regularly pay an
insurance company an amount of money so that they will
give you money if something you own is damaged, lost or
stolen, or if you die or are ill or injured. *Investigation* is the
process of trying to find out all the details or facts about
something in order to discover who or what caused it or
how it happened. James Bond tells Scaramanga that he is in
Jamaica to find out all the details about the fires affecting the
sugar cane crops for an insurance company.

25 **freelance** (page 30)

freelance work is done by a person who is not permanently
employed by a particular company but who sells their services
to more than one company

26 **share** (page 30)

one of the equal parts of a company that you can buy as a
way of investing money. People who have invested money in
shares are called *shareholders*.

27 **dozen** (page 30)

a set of twelve things or people. *Half a dozen* means six.

28 **bug** – *to bug something* (page 31)

to hide a small piece of electronic equipment somewhere so
that you can secretly listen to what people are saying

29 **booby trap** (page 33)

a trick that is designed to catch someone. Bond's *booby trap*
will tell him if somebody tries to enter his room.

30 **mangrove swamp** (page 34)

a *mangrove* is a tropical tree that grows beside water and
has roots that begin above the ground. These trees grow in
swamps or *swampland* – areas of land covered by water where
trees and plants grow.

31 **tax concession** (page 34)

a reduction in the rate of taxes for some groups of people

32 **syndicate** (page 34)

a group of people or organizations that work together and share the cost of a particular business that needs a large amount of money

33 **one-armed bandit** (page 35)

a machine that you put money into in order to play a game, especially in a casino

34 **Mafia** (page 38)

a secret criminal organization involved in illegal activities in Italy and the USA

35 **undercover** (page 39)

someone who is working *undercover* is pretending to be someone else in order to find out secret information

36 **the CIA** (page 39)

the Central Intelligence Agency: a US government organization that collects secret information about other countries and protects secret information about the USA

37 **relieved** (page 39)

happy and relaxed because something bad has not happened or because a bad situation has ended

38 **sabotage** (page 41)

deliberate damage that is done to the property of an enemy or opponent

39 **futures** (page 41)

agreements to buy or sell shares, goods or currency. The price is agreed in advance – before the time in the future when the shares or goods will be delivered.

40 **sugar lobby** (page 41)

a *lobby* is an organized group of people who represent a particular area of business or society and try to influence politicians. The *sugar lobby* is concerned with the production, buying and selling of sugar.

41 **loan** (page 43)

an amount of money that a person, business or country borrows, especially from a bank

42 **mortgage** (page 43)

a legal agreement in which you borrow money from a bank in order to buy a house or other property. You pay back your mortgage by making monthly payments.

43 **fuse** (page 45)

a part of a piece of electrical equipment that makes it stop working when there is too much electricity flowing through it

44 **got rid of** – *to get rid of something* (page 45)

to throw away, give away or sell something that you no longer want or need. Scaramanga plans to throw the body of the dead man into the swamp.

45 **paid off** – *to pay off* (page 48)

if something that you do *pays off*, it brings you some benefit

46 **shown off** – *to show off* (page 48)

you *show off* when you behave in a way that shows people that you are very proud of something that you can do or that you have done, so that they will admire you

47 **rare** (page 54)

rare meat has been cooked for only a short time and is red inside

48 **spring** (page 55)

a long, thin piece of metal that is curved or *coiled* into circles and which quickly gets its original shape back again after you stop stretching it

49 **replica** (page 56)

an accurate copy of something

50 **coal-tender** (page 56)

the part of a train that contains the fuel and water for a steam engine

51 **shop window dummy** (page 59)

a model of a human body, used especially in the window of a shop to display clothes that are for sale

52 **buffer** (page 59)

one of two metal springs at the front and back of a train and at the end of a railway line that helps to protect the train if it crashes

53 **clearing** (page 63)

an area in a forest where there are no trees or bushes

54 **pulse** (page 68)

the regular movement of blood as the heart pumps it round the body. The rate of someone's *pulse* is the number of movements that you can feel in a minute when you put your finger on their skin over a blood vessel.

55 **crutch** (page 69)

a stick that you lean on when your leg or foot is injured so that you can walk

56 **judicial inquiry** (page 70)

an official examination of a crime, accident, problem, etc. carried out by a judge or court, in order to get information or the truth

57 **sealed** – *to seal something* (page 71)

to close an envelope or packet by sticking down the top edge or wrapping. Sometimes, *sealing wax* – a hard substance that becomes like a liquid when you heat it – is used to make a *seal*. You have to break it before you can open the letter, document, packet, etc. *Seals* are used especially on official or secret documents and packages.

58 **gallant and meritorious services** (page 72)

work or duties done for a person or an organization which are brave and deserve admiration and praise. This medal is awarded to Bond for his work to help the Jamaican government. *Gallant* is a literary word meaning brave. *Meritorious* is a very formal word used to describe actions which deserve admiration.

59 **knighthood** (page 75)

an honour given by a British king or queen that allows a man to use the title 'Sir' before his name

60 **KCMG** (page 75)

the Most Distinguished Order of Saint Michael and Saint George: a medal awarded by a British king or queen to someone who has done something very brave in another country which is under British control. Bond has already received this medal for work he has done in the past.

61 *peasant* (page 75)

a poor person who works on a farm. *Peasant* is sometimes used in an offensive way to describe someone who is poor, uneducated and from a low social class. This is the meaning that Bond uses here. He is saying that he is proud of being from a low social class and does not want to change his social position by accepting the knighthood and becoming Sir James Bond.

Useful Phrases

Long time no see (page 14)
used when you meet someone who you have not seen for a long time

press any charges – *to press charges* (page 16)
to officially accuse someone of committing a crime

has the nerve – *to have the nerve to do something* (page 16)
to have a rude attitude, usually shown by behaviour that makes other people angry

signed James Bond's death warrant – *to sign someone's death warrant* (page 20)
to do something that will cause someone great danger or very serious problems. M is afraid that by sending Bond on this mission he will cause his death.

kill time – *to kill time* (page 20)
to make time seem to pass more quickly by doing something instead of just waiting

could not believe his eyes (page 21)
used for emphasizing that you are extremely surprised or angry about something you have seen

What on earth …? – *what / how / why on earth …?* (page 22)
used for adding emphasis to questions

give me a hard time – *to give someone a hard time* (page 27)
to be unpleasant to someone, make a situation more difficult for them or criticize them a lot

We could do with you – *could do with something* (page 28)
used for saying that you want or need something

Do you get me? (page 31)
used for saying 'Do you understand me?'

nosing around – *to nose around* (page 31)
to try to find out information about someone or something. This expression shows disapproval of someone's behaviour.

get a good picture of – *to get a good picture of something* (page 34)
to get a good understanding of something or see it clearly

making small talk – *to make small talk* (page 37)
to have an informal conversation about things that are not important

stopped in his tracks – *to stop in your tracks* (page 39)
to suddenly stop, for example because you are surprised

we have them cornered – *to have someone cornered* (page 41)
to be in control of a situation so that someone has to do what you want them to do

in the red (page 42)
with more money being spent than there is available

Not on your life! (page 43)
used for telling someone that you will certainly not do something

breathed a sigh of relief – *to breathe a sigh of relief* (page 49)
to stop worrying because something bad is no longer likely to happen

at all costs (page 49)
used for saying that something must be done, however difficult it is or however much damage it causes

put two and two together – *to put two and two together* (page 49)
to guess what is happening or what something means as a result of what you have seen or heard

weighing up the evidence – *to weigh up the evidence* (page 52)
to think about the evidence carefully

give him the edge – *to give someone the edge* (page 55)
to give someone or something an advantage that makes them more successful than other people or things

That'll be the day! (page 61)
used for saying that you do not believe something will ever happen

the end of the road (page 63)
the moment when someone or something has to stop, for example because they cannot succeed or improve

Glossary and Useful Phrases definitions adapted from the Macmillan English Dictionary 2ⁿᵈ *Edition*
© *Macmillan Publishers Limited 2007* www.macmillandictionary.com

Exercises

Background Information

Read 'A Note About The Author' and 'A Note About The Story'. Match the topics on the left with the details on the right.

1	Born	a	Eton
2	Died	b	one
3	Education	c	until 1958
4	Fleming in Moscow	d	28th May 1908
5	Fleming in London	e	1974
6	Second World War	f	fifteen
7	Children	g	Fidel Castro
8	First novel	h	Caribbean island
9	Number of 007 books	i	1964
10	Film version of this book	j	banker and broker
11	The Cold War	k	KGB
12	The Soviet Union	l	Reuters
13	Soviet secret police	m	Fulgencio Batista
14	Jamaica	n	communist Russia and other countries
15	Under British rule	o	1962
16	Ex-ruler of Cuba	p	1952
17	Communist Prime Minister of Cuba	q	1945–1989
18	Cuban missile crisis	r	Naval Intelligence

People in the Story

Write a name from the box next to the correct information below.

> Felix Leiter   Hendriks   ~~James Bond~~   Mary Goodnight
> Nick Nicholson   Ruby Rotkopf   Scaramanga   Tiffy

1   _James Bond_   is a British Secret Service employee.

2   .... is Ross's secretary.

3   .... is working for the Cuban secret police.

4   .... is a CIA employee.

5   .... is the manager of the Dreamland Café.

6   .... is working for the KGB.

7   .... is a CIA expert in electronics.

8   .... is a hotel owner.

True or False

Read the sentences about events in the story. Write T (True) or F (False).

1   James Bond was held prisoner in Japan.   _F_

2   The KGB sent James Bond to kill M.   ....

3   M ordered Bond to find and kill Scaramanga.   ....

4   Scaramanga learnt how to use guns in the army.   ....

5   After six months, Bond discovered where to find Scaramanga.   ....

6   Mary Goodnight gave Bond money and a gun.   ....

7   James Bond met Scaramanga in the Dreamland Café.   ....

8   Scaramanga offered Bond a job as the hotel manager.   ....

9   James Bond met Felix Leiter, who was working at the hotel.
   ....

95

10 Scaramanga killed one of his business partners. ....

11 Mary Goodnight visited Bond to give him a warning. ....

12 Hendriks knew Bond's real identity. ....

13 Mary Goodnight was run over by a train. ....

14 Felix Leiter put a bomb under the bridge. ....

15 Bond killed Scaramanga. ....

16 The Police Commissioner supported the actions of Bond and Leiter. ....

17 James Bond accepted an award from the Queen. ....

Multiple Choice

Tick the best answer.

1 Bond tried to kill M using
   a bullets.
   b a knife.
   c poisonous gas. ✓

2 The Cuban sugar crop was much smaller than usual because of
   a fires.
   b the weather.
   c Fidel Castro.

3 Scaramanga could not finish building the hotel because
   a there was a war.
   b tourists had stopped going there.
   c the investors did not have any more money.

4 American businessmen bought property in Jamaica because
   a it was cheap.
   b they could sell it for a high price.
   c they did not have to pay as much tax.

5 Ruby Rotkopf was killed because
   a he wanted to take out a second mortgage.
   b he did not want to give any more money to build the hotel.
   c he was a lawyer.

6 Mary Goodnight told Bond that
   a he should go to Havana.
   b the police wanted to arrest him.
   c Hendriks was there to kill him.

7 Hendriks was angry with Scaramanga for
   a letting Bond get too close.
   b not doing anything about the aluminium industry.
   c killing Rotkopf.

8 Leiter said he would stay on the train
   a to make sure the other men were arrested.
   b to kill the other men himself.
   c to make sure the bomb exploded.

9 Scaramanga thought that Bond would not kill him because Bond
   a was injured.
   b was British.
   c had respect for the law.

10 Bond was worried because
   a he had not killed Scaramanga.
   b the Jamaican police knew all about his mission.
   c he had not talked to Leiter before the inquiry.

11 Bond did not accept the award from the Queen because
   a being famous was not important to him.
   b he was Welsh.
   c he thought awards were stupid.

Vocabulary: Spying

Complete the gaps. Use each word in the box once.

> assassin booby traps brainwashed bug bulletproof
> ~~devices~~ poison sabotage sedatives tortured
> trace a call undercover

During the Cold War, organizations such as the KGB, CIA and
British Secret Service used special (1) _____*devices*_____ to
(2) _____ the plans of their enemies because they
wanted those plans to fail. In order to find out information,
agents used to (3) _____ rooms or phones to listen
to what people were talking about. They also used equipment
to (4) _____ if they wanted to discover where the
telephone call was coming from. Sometimes, agents went
(5) _____ and pretended they were working for their
enemy. They sometimes used (6) _____, which could
harm or kill people when they did not expect there to be any
danger. If agents were captured, they were (7) _____
to try to make them give useful, secret information to their
enemy. This physical violence was sometimes accompanied by
mental abuse. Captured agents could be (8) _____
to make them believe the enemy was right and their old
organization was wrong. They were given (9) _____
as part of this process. If someone important became too
dangerous, an (10) _____ was sent to kill him. This
could be done with (11) _____, which could be put
in a drink or food. To protect themselves from gunshots while
they were driving, agents' cars had (12) _____ glass
windows.

Vocabulary: Definitions

Match the words and definitions.

1 villain	a	sticks that help you walk
2 democracy	b	very soft, wet land
3 conference	c	someone you compete against
4 penultimate	d	a criminal
5 missile	e	second from last
6 ruthless	f	an exact copy of something
7 rival	g	money you borrow from a bank to buy a house
8 syndicate	h	a system in which people vote in elections
9 swampland	i	a group of businessmen sharing the cost
10 mortgage	j	the pumping of blood round the body
11 replica	k	willing to cause pain and suffering
12 pulse	l	a meeting to discuss a particular topic
13 crutches	m	twelve
14 dozen	n	a flying weapon

Complete the sentences with one of the words from the table.

15 Scaramanga was a .... killer and did not feel sorry for what he did to others.

16 Leiter's leg was broken in several places and he had to use ....

17 November is the .... month of the year.

18 Scaramanga created a .... to raise money to build a hotel.

19 He held a .... at the hotel to discuss the situation.

20 Rotkopf's body was put in the .... , where the crocodiles would find it.

Word Focus

Choose the correct word to complete the sentences.

1 Scaramanga had put a <u>dead body</u> / (dummy) on the train track to trick Bond.

2 Scaramanga wanted to <u>get rid of / pay off</u> Bond. He wanted to kill him.

3 Bond told Scaramanga that he was <u>freelance / a labourer</u> and that he worked for himself.

4 Although Bond took some risks, they <u>showed off / paid off</u> because they had good results.

5 The Secret Service developed specialist equipment in <u>a laboratory / a clearing</u>.

6 All the gang members had bought <u>parts / shares</u> in the hotel.

Useful Phrases

Replace the underlined words with phrases from the box.

> brought / up to date   could do with   couldn't believe his eyes
> have them cornered   in his tracks   ~~kill time~~
> made small talk   Not on your life!   That'll be the day!
> Why on earth are you here?

1 Bond looked at the shops to <u>make the time seem shorter</u>
  before his flight. _____ *kill time*

2 Bond <u>was very surprised at what he saw</u>.
  ....

3 <u>I'm very surprised you've come here to the hotel</u>.
  ....

4 Mary Goodnight <u>gave</u> Bond <u>the most recent information</u>.
  ....

5 We <u>need</u> a man like you.
  ....

6 Bond <u>talked about unimportant things</u> with the gangsters.
  ....

7 Bond stopped <u>what he was doing</u> when he saw Leiter.
  ....

8 We <u>have made it impossible for them to refuse us</u>.
  ....

9 I won't pay more – <u>definitely not</u>!
  ....

10 Will Bond ever get hurt? <u>I'll be surprised</u>!
  ....

Grammar: Reporting verbs

Rewrite the sentences with the verbs in the box. You may need to change the form of the verbs.

> accuse   admit   order   refuse   warn

1 'Sit outside the door, Bond.'

Scaramanga _____ *ordered Bond to sit outside the door*.

2 'We have made mistakes.'

Scaramanga _____

3 'You must be careful, James.'

Mary Goodnight _____

4 'Put your hands behind your head, Scaramanga!'

Leiter _____

5 'I won't take part in it!'

Rotkopf _____

6 'Watch what you're saying, Bond.'

Scaramanga _____

7 'You killed my friends, Scaramanga.'

Bond _____

8 'We have run out of money.'

Scaramanga _____

9 'Open your jacket slowly, Scaramanga.'

Bond _____

10 'You are just making money for yourselves.'

Hendriks _____

Grammar: Past perfect simple and continuous

Choose the correct verb form, past perfect simple or continuous, to complete the sentences.

1 Before he found the note at the airport, Bond had looked / had been looking for Scaramanga for six weeks.

2 He had been booking / had booked a flight to Cuba but had to cancel it.

3 Bond had known / had been knowing Mary for years.

4 Before telephoning M, Bond had been buying / had bought a new suit.

5 Mary had been finding out / had found out where Bond was from Tiffy.

6 She had warned / had been warning Bond about Hendriks.

7 They had been talking / had talked in the bathroom when they were surprised by Scaramanga.

8 They had been seeing / had seen the body on the track too late to stop.

9 Felix had been hiding / had hidden on the train for some time.

10 Scaramanga had murdered / had been murdering nearly fifty people.

Pronunciation: Word stress

Write the words in the correct column of the table.

> assassin atomic democracy insurance intercom
> judicial laboratory penultimate sedative syndicates

● ● ●	● ● ●	● ● ● ●
	assassin	

Macmillan Education
Between Towns Road, Oxford OX4 3PP
A division of Macmillan Publishers Limited
Companies and representatives throughout the world

ISBN 978–0–230–42228–5
ISBN 978–0–230–42234–6 (with CD edition)

Designed by Carolyn Gibson
Illustrated by Paul McCaffrey
Cover photograph by Superstock/Corbis

Printed and bound in Thailand

without CD edition

2018	2017	2016	2015	2014	2013
10	9	8	7	6	5	4	3	2	1

with CD edition

2018	2017	2016	2015	2014	2013
10	9	8	7	6	5	4	3	2	1